TURN IT UP

TURN IT UP

a VARSITY novel

by Melanie Spring

poppy

Little, Brown and Company

New York Boston

Copyright © 2014 by Varsity Spirit Corporation
Varsity is a registered trademark of Varsity Spirit Corporation.

Poppy

Hachette Book Group
237 Park Avenue, New York, NY 10017
Visit our website at lb-teens.com

Poppy is an imprint of Little, Brown and Company.
The Poppy name and logo are trademarks of Hachette Book Group, Inc.

The publisher is not responsible for websites (or their content) that are not owned
by the publisher.

First Edition: May 2014

Library of Congress Cataloging-in-Publication Data

Spring, Melanie.
Turn it up : a Varsity novel / by Melanie Spring. — First edition.
pages cm
"Poppy."
Sequel to: Game on.
Summary: "Fourteen-year-old JV cheerleaders Chloe, Kate, Emily, and Devin return as the Timberwolves prepare for Nationals amidst the dramas of best friends, boyfriends, and freshman year at Northside High in Southern California"— Provided by publisher.
ISBN 978-0-316-22724-7 (pbk.) — ISBN 978-0-316-22723-0 (e-book)
[1. Cheerleading—Fiction. 2. Best friends—Fiction. 3. Friendship—Fiction.
4. High schools—Fiction. 5. Schools—Fiction.] I. Title.
PZ7.S76843Tur 2014 [Fic]—dc23 2013022846

10 9 8 7 6 5 4 3 2 1

RRD-C

Printed in the United States of America

TURN IT UP

CHAPTER 1

Chloe Davis smoothed her gold NHS CHEER T-shirt over her blue camp shorts as she strode into the Northside High gym, swinging her duffel bag. She was eager to get started with the first Junior Varsity practice of the new year, especially after having been away for the holidays. Her family's ski trip to Aspen had been a blast, but cheering was the center of her universe. Moguls were cool. Liberties were even better!

Glancing around, Chloe noticed that the gym had been spruced up over the two-week break. New banners hung above the basketball backboards: HOME OF THE TIMBERWOLVES in blue letters, NORTHSIDE PRIDE in gold.

The floor had been refinished and looked extra-shiny and glossy, the color of maple syrup.

"*Chloooeee!*" Emily Arellano practically tackled her from behind in a crushing bear hug. Emily was one of Chloe's best friends. Her long, wavy dark hair was pulled back in a high pony, and the only adornment on her flawless olive face was a temporary tattoo on her cheek: a Timberwolf paw.

"*Ow!* I'm happy to see you, too," Chloe said, laughing. "What's up with the tattoo? Our game's not till Friday."

"I'm getting into the spirit early! How was your trip? Why weren't you in school today? Are you sick? You aren't sick, are you?" Emily jerked back and looked Chloe up and down suspiciously.

"We were supposed to fly home yesterday, but our flight was delayed. Mom drove me to school right before sixth period," Chloe replied, brushing back her strawberry-blond bangs.

"Oh. I texted you, like, a zillion times, but you didn't text back," Emily complained.

"I'm sorry! I lost my phone in the snow. Dad's getting me a replacement tonight—an upgrade."

"Must be nice. Santa didn't bring me an iPhone this year, like I totally asked for, so I'm stuck with Chad." Emily held up her ancient purple cell with the faded heart stickers on it. Chad was her nickname for it. "Can you believe

I can't even video chat on it? It's totally prehistoric," she sniped.

"Put that away! What if Coach walks in and sees you?" Chloe warned. Coach Steele had a lot of rules for the squad, and "No phones during practice" was one of her top five.

Emily rolled her brown eyes and tucked Chad into the pocket of her Northside hoodie. It was common knowledge that she wasn't a big fan of rules. Luckily, Coach Steele was nowhere in sight. She was probably off creating one of her famous action plans for today's session.

Chloe and Emily linked arms and headed over to the bleachers together. Chloe spotted Kalyn Min, Jenn Hoffheimer, Lexi Foster, and Carley Chase-Calloway doing hamstring stretches on the mats. Marcy Martinez and Arianna Clark were gabbing and putting their hair up into high ponies with shiny white ribbons. The rest of the squad practiced double toe touches in the corner.

"Oooooh, I see Leila over there. Is it my imagination, or did her skin finally turn orange? Must be all that spray-tanning," Emily remarked as she set her duffel bag down on a bench.

Chloe stifled a giggle. "Em, be nice!"

"Because Leila is so nice to us? Yeah, I don't think so," Emily said sarcastically.

Chloe and Leila Savett used to be good friends. In elementary school and middle school, they had baked cookies together and carpooled to the mall. On Saturdays, they had trained together at a cheerleading gym called Sunny Valley All-Stars.

But when Chloe made the elite team at the gym and Leila didn't, things changed dramatically. Since then Leila had made it her personal mission to make Chloe's life miserable. Back in September, she'd even tried to destroy Chloe's chance at becoming JV captain.

Lucky for Chloe, Leila hadn't succeeded.

"Hi, Chloe! You're back!"

Chloe turned. Kate MacDonald rushed up and gave her a quick, affectionate hug. Kate was one of Chloe's other best friends. She wore a pale green T-shirt that complemented her dark hair; there was a Disney Princess Band-Aid stuck to the hem, probably put there by one of her younger siblings. Devin Isle trailed behind, her face creased in a frown as she tried to pull her wild red curls into a ponytail. Devin was Chloe's cocaptain on the team.

"Hi, Kate! Hi, Devin!" Chloe said with a smile.

"How was Aspen?" Kate asked, adjusting her shorts over her long legs.

"It was perfect! It was nice to spend time with Jake and Clementine. Well, except for this one night when they put a plastic snake in my bed, and I thought it was real." Chloe's twin sibs were seniors in college, but they still acted like they were in elementary school sometimes. "How was your vacation?" she asked Kate.

"Kinda quiet," Kate said, grabbing her elbows above her head to stretch her triceps. "I reread all my favorite Jane Austen books." Kate was a freshman, like Chloe, Emily, and Devin, but she took a lot of advanced classes, and she was always reading classic novels.

"Hello? What about our epic horror-movie-marathon sleepover?" Emily reminded Kate.

Devin grinned. "Oh, yeah. I'm still having nightmares about those slimy green space zombies."

"Eww, me too," Kate said with a shudder.

Chloe's smile wavered. Emily and Kate had a sleepover without her? And they'd invited the new girl, Devin?

Granted, Devin wasn't exactly the new girl anymore. And she and Chloe had worked out their differences after their difficult, drama-filled start as cocaptains.

Back in September, Devin had joined the team without so much as a tryout just because Coach Steele was good friends with Devin's mom, and because Devin was a talented tumbler. To make things worse, Devin had been elected cocaptain even though Chloe was clearly meant to be the *sole* captain.

For months, Chloe and Devin had struggled back and forth on how to lead the team. Leila hadn't helped, sending a fake e-mail trashing Devin and pretending that Chloe had written it.

But now they were okay. Sort of. They weren't best friends, exactly, but they weren't fighting anymore, either.

Chloe forced herself to put on a brave, cheerful face as Devin, Emily, and Kate gabbed about their sleepover. Jealousy wasn't her thing. And it wasn't as though Emily and Kate had replaced her with Devin. The three of them had been best friends since they picked up their first poms together in sixth grade. Their bond was unshakable.

"So, Devin! Your boyfriend flew down for New Year's Eve, right?" Chloe asked in a friendly voice.

"Yeah. I was super-happy to see him," Devin said distractedly.

Chloe didn't know how to translate that. Devin didn't *sound* super-happy. Devin and her boyfriend, Josh, had been long-distance since she'd moved to Sunny Valley six months earlier. Shouldn't she have been ecstatic about spending a romantic holiday with him?

But Devin didn't seem to want to talk about it. "So are we all ready for Nationals?" she said, changing the subject.

"Yes!" Emily thrust her arms up in the air.

"No," Kate said at the same time. "I haven't nailed my back handspring yet. Ugh."

"We're staying at Disney's All-Star Sports Resort, right? I Googled it—it looks cool," Devin remarked.

Chloe still couldn't believe the Northside JV cheer squad had come in second at Regionals back in November, qualifying them for Nationals. Devin had actually played a big part in that, stepping up to lead the team when Chloe sprained her ankle.

The thought of competing against the top cheerleading teams in the country filled Chloe with excitement. And fear. Fortunately, the event was taking place at Disney World near Orlando, Florida. *If we fail, at least we can have some fun,* she thought.

"I can't wait to ride the Tower of Terror," Chloe said out loud. "I heard there's gonna be a ton of cool stuff at registration, too. A red carpet, an awesome gift shop—"

"Don't forget hot guys," Emily finished with a sly grin.

"The Tower of Terror? Hot guys? Ladies, let's get our priorities in order."

Chloe and her friends whirled around. Coach Steele stood there, holding her action plan binder in one hand and a silver coffee thermos in the other. With her short brown hair, gold-accented navy warm-ups, and sleek white running shoes, she looked like the epitome of a professional cheer coach.

"Hi, Coach! We were just...um..." Emily stammered.

"Yes, I know what you were just, um, doing," Coach Steele said wryly. "Vacation's over, my little Timberwolves. We have exactly thirty-three days to prepare for Nationals.

So let's stop goofing around and get to work. Are you ready?"

"Yes, Coach!" Chloe, Emily, Kate, and Devin replied in unison.

"Chloe and Devin, are you ready to lead this team to victory?" Coach Steele barked.

"*Yes, Coach!*" Chloe and Devin shouted.

Coach Steele reached for the whistle around her neck and blew it, hard. All the cheerleaders in the gym stopped what they were doing, scrambled to their feet, and gathered around their coach in a wide semicircle.

"Welcome back, ladies! It's nice to see all of your bright, shining faces," Coach Steele called out. "We have a lot to do between now and February eighth. Your routine is good, but it needs to be great. And at the moment, it's far from that."

"*Ouch,*" Emily muttered under her breath.

"In Orlando, you will need to impress a panel of judges who are used to seeing the best of the best," Coach Steele went on. "You, my lovely Wolves, will need to electrify. You will need to project. You will *not* be performing for a few hundred hometown fans at a basketball game. You will be performing for ten thousand strangers in a huge arena that's three, four, *five* times the size of our gymnasium. And make no mistake—most of these strangers have their own schools to root for. They won't be cheering for you."

"Did she say *ten thousand*?" Devin whispered to Chloe.

Chloe gulped and nodded.

"This is the big league, ladies," Coach Steele continued. "We need to turn it up. Are you with me?"

"*Yes, Coach!*" all eighteen cheerleaders shouted.

"Timber! Timber! Timber-wolves!" Chloe chanted, pumping her fists in the air.

The other girls joined in: "Timber! Timber! Timber-wolves!"

Coach Steele nodded approvingly. Then she raised her hands, and the chanting ceased abruptly. "I'm glad we're all on the same page. And while we're on the subject of turning it up...I wanted to let you know that we will be adding weekend practices to our schedule for the next four weeks. I'll be announcing dates and times shortly, as soon as I've had a chance to confer with Principal Cilento. Now, everyone give me ten laps and twenty push-ups! After that, we'll be breaking up into groups to practice our stunts."

Weekend practices? "Did you know anything about this?" Chloe whispered to Devin.

Devin shook her head.

"Good-bye, fun!" Emily said glumly.

"Farewell, sleeping in!" Kate added.

As she started to jog, Chloe thought about Coach Steele's words. Nationals called for a whole new level of performance, and preparing for it had to be the number one priority in their lives. Chloe had to make sure to keep her teammates' spirits up and everyone's motivation high.

Chloe rounded the first corner of the gym. She passed Gemma Moore running alone. Like Chloe, Gemma was a freshman.

Chloe slowed down while Emily and the others continued on, discussing their busy schedules. "Hi, Gemma. How's your standing tuck coming along? Maybe I can help you with it later," Chloe called out.

Gemma didn't reply.

Glancing over, Chloe realized that her teammate's face was red and blotchy, as though she'd been crying.

"Omigosh, Gemma! Are you okay? What's the—"

Before Chloe could finish her sentence, Gemma redoubled her speed and took off in a fast sprint.

What's wrong with Gemma? Chloe wondered.

CHAPTER 2

"Sweetie, can you please pass the garlic bread?"

Emily grabbed two big pieces of garlic bread from the basket before passing it around the table to her mother, Irene Arellano. Monday was spaghetti night, Emily's favorite.

"Uh, could you save some for the rest of us?" her older brother Chris complained. He was a senior at Northside High and a forward for the Varsity basketball team.

"Hey, you've already had, like, five," Emily pointed out.

"Yeah, well, I had a tough practice today," Chris told her.

"Yeah, well, me too!"

"You two keep arguing. I'll just finish that up," their

brother, Eddie, said, grabbing the basket. Eddie lived at home and worked as a barista at a local café called the Mighty Cup. He was also studying business at Sunny Valley Community College.

"Seriously? The three of you? There's more garlic bread in the kitchen, so stop squabbling," Mrs. Arellano said, laughing.

"I made two extra loaves. I've learned from past Mondays," Mr. Arellano piped up.

"Papi, you rock," Emily told him. Jose Arellano worked two jobs—as a mechanic and a security guard—and yet he always seemed to find the time to prepare the family dinners. Mrs. Arellano, who was a preschool teacher, hated to cook. When they got married, they'd made a deal that he would be in charge of the kitchen and she would be in charge of the rest of the house. They also held hands and often said "*te amo*" to each other, which Emily teased them about. Secretly, though, she was happy that they were so happy. After all, Kate's parents were divorced, and so were Devin's.

"So how was practice today, Emily? Did Coach Steele make you guys go over the dance?" Mrs. Arellano asked.

"And how are the stunts coming along?" Mr. Arellano added. The Arellanos had always been super-involved in Northside athletics, including the cheer program. They knew Emily's routines almost as well as she did.

Emily made a face. "Practice was brutal. The dance is

hard, and so are the stunts. Plus, Coach made us do tumbling passes until our legs were practically falling off."

"Nationals is just around the corner and the practices are going to get even tougher. You'll need to pace yourself," Mrs. Arellano advised.

"Yeah, but how? Coach just told us that she's adding weekend practices. That's on top of our regular practices on Mondays, Tuesdays, and Wednesdays, tumbling gym on Thursdays, and games on Fridays," Emily rattled off. "*Plus*, there's school. *Plus*, I'm in charge of the Valentine's Day dance this year. *Plus*, I have to come up with an idea for our big fund-raiser on January twenty-fifth. We need to raise more money for Nationals and for charity."

The squad held fund-raisers several times a year, with half of the money going to competition fees and other expenses, and the other half going to a charity of their choice. Last fall, they'd held a bake sale, and the proceeds had gone to Regionals fees and a local nonprofit organization called Hearts Heal. Before Christmas, Emily had promised Coach Steele and the other cheerleaders that she'd organize the winter fund-raiser, and she couldn't back out now.

Emily had also served on the homecoming dance committee. After the success of that event, the other members had elected her to chair the Valentine's Day dance effort, and she'd said yes to that as well.

On top of it all, Emily sang with her friend Travis Hollister's band, Hashtag, once in a while. In fact, she was due at Travis's house after dinner for an "emergency band meeting," whatever that meant.

Just saying her to-do list out loud made Emily feel exhausted. How was she going to accomplish everything? Fortunately, she liked being busy, and she tended to thrive under pressure. She'd just have to make sure to take a lot of mental-health breaks with her friends. *And* drink more coffee.

Mr. Arellano reached over and squeezed Emily's hand. "You can do it, sweetie. But don't take on any more commitments, okay? You've got enough on your plate."

"Okay." Emily hesitated. "I told Travis I could go to his house later, though. Can anyone give me a ride?"

Mrs. Arellano raised her eyebrows. "Band practice on a school night?"

"No, not practice! We're having a meeting. It'll take, like, half an hour, forty minutes, tops. I finished my homework already, in study hall," Emily said quickly.

Her parents exchanged a glance. "Half an hour, okay? Chris can take you, and I'll pick you up," Mr. Arellano said.

"Wait, what? Don't I get a say in this?" Chris protested.

"Honey, you should seriously consider putting the band on hold until after Nationals," Mrs. Arellano told Emily.

"Remember when Chris's team was getting ready for State last year? And Eddie's team before that? It was nonstop practices—and nonstop pressure, too."

"I know, I know," Emily conceded. Maybe her parents were right. Maybe she should tell Travis that she wanted to take a break for a while.

✻

Emily wiggled around in the massive beanbag chair, trying to find a comfortable center. The Hollisters' basement decor was a teen guy's dream, with its vintage Beatles posters, Ping-Pong table, and collection of musical instruments, including a white drum set.

"So what's the big emergency?" Alex Guzmann asked. He was sprawled out on the brown corduroy couch, plucking his bass. One of his sneakers was purple and the other, green.

"Yeah. I still have to study for Mr. Reaser's quiz," Kyle Klein, the drummer, added. "On functions. Who gives quizzes the Tuesday after vacation, right?" Like Alex and Travis, Kyle was a junior.

"Forget about the functions quiz, nerd. You're not going to need precalc when you're rocking the stage at the Hollywood Bowl in front of eighteen thousand screaming fans," Travis said.

Kyle's eyes widened. "Excuse me?"

Travis grinned. "Remember Nic Aragon?"

"Nic Aragon?" Emily sat up straight—or tried to, anyway. *Stupid beanbag chair.* Nic Aragon was a talent scout who'd invited Hashtag to make a demo last fall. Emily had come *this close* to missing Regionals because the recording session had taken place on the same exact day, in Los Angeles, at SV Studios.

But that was back in November, and they hadn't heard from Nic since then. Talent scouts were supposed to seek out groups like Hashtag and hook them up with record companies. Did Travis finally have some news?

"Well?" Alex demanded.

"Yeah, spill," Kyle added.

"Two words. Rampage. Records," Travis said slowly.

Alex raised his eyebrows. "Rampage Records? Calla's label?"

Calla? *The* Calla? Emily practically fell out of her beanbag chair. The bad-girl pop star from Belfast, Ireland, was one of her favorite singers ever.

Travis nodded. "Calla, the Blue Skinks, Indianapolis, Soul Alignment...you name it. Nick shared our demo with Jacinta Cruz, who's, like, one of the big executives at Rampage. Nic says they might be interested in signing us up."

Emily's breath caught in her throat. Signing up...as in a recording contract? This was *huge*.

"We're gonna be famous!" Alex yelled.

"We're gonna be rich!" Kyle picked up a pair of drumsticks and played a riff on the cymbals.

The basement door opened. "Can you rich-and-famous rock stars lower the volume? We're trying to get the baby to sleep," Mrs. Hollister called down the stairs.

"Sorry, Mom!" Travis replied. "So," he said to the group. "Next step. Nic said Jacinta wants us to write and record a couple more songs. I'm gonna drive to Los Angeles this weekend to meet with her and get more details. Does anyone have ideas for new material?"

As the three guys discussed song ideas, Emily tried to digest what was happening. A meeting in LA. Recording sessions. A possible contract. This was a dream come true for any high school band.

Of course, Emily wasn't an official Hashtag member. She sang with them from time to time, when they needed a female vocalist, but Rampage Records was probably just interested in the three main guys. She was really happy for them and not in the least bit envious.

Well, maybe a *little* envious.

At eight o'clock on the dot, Mr. Arellano texted Emily—he was waiting for her outside. Emily said goodbye to Alex and Kyle, and Travis walked her upstairs.

In the dimly lit hallway, Emily grabbed her jean jacket from the coatrack. Travis put his hand on her shoulder and said: "Wait up. I want to talk to you."

"Sure. About what?"

"About the big news. What do you think?"

"I think it's totally amazing! Congratulations!" Emily replied.

"Um, well...congratulations to you, too! You're part of this," Travis told her.

"Not exactly. I mean, I'm not even in the band. Not officially, anyway," Emily hedged.

Travis grinned. "So let's make it official. I now pronounce you a member of Hashtag. Problem solved."

"Wow. Thank you. I'm really, really flattered." Emily hesitated. "The thing is, I have a zillion other things going on right now. My parents told me I have to cut back on extracurricular activities."

Travis regarded her with his green eyes. His *nice* green eyes that went so well with his blond hair, which was super-short, except for the long bangs that fell across his face. Paired with his black NHS JAZZ BAND T-shirt and dark skinny jeans, Travis was pretty cute, in an emo sort of way. Why hadn't she noticed before?

"Emily, you should know that Nic told me that Rampage liked the songs with your vocals on it the best," Travis said.

Emily gasped. "Omigod, really?"

"Really. Hashtag needs you." Travis paused. "*I* need you."

His hand slid from her shoulder to her elbow to her wrist, and it lingered there lightly. His touch on her bare skin was warm and intimate.

Emily's heart skipped a beat as she extracted her hand from Travis's and took a step back. Why was he having this effect on her all of a sudden? They were friends. Besides which, he totally wasn't her type. She liked jocks, not band geeks. Lacrosse stars, not guitar players.

"Come to LA with me on Sunday?" Travis asked.

I can't, she thought.

But before she could stop herself, she opened her mouth and said, "Okay."

She really had to learn to say no one of these days.

CHAPTER 3

"So what classes do you have this morning?" Devin asked Josh—or rather, the image of Josh on her laptop screen, complete with sun-streaked blond hair, light blue eyes, and surfer-boy tan. In the background, she could see that his room was a total disaster, as always: bed unmade, clothes strewn across the floor, his acoustic guitar, which he called Lucy, propped precariously against an overflowing trash can. The two of them were squeezing in an early Skype session before they had to leave for their respective schools: Northside High for her and Spring Park High for him, hundreds of miles north.

Before, when people asked Devin where she went to

school, she would say, "Spring Park." Then she'd correct herself: *I used to go there, but my mom and I moved down here last summer. My sister, Sage, is a sophomore at UCLA, and we wanted to be closer to her. Plus, there's the whole divorce thing. My parents split up, and my mom, she's a nurse, she wanted to start over somewhere brand-new...*

Lately, though, she hadn't had that problem. When Devin thought about school, she thought about Northside. When she thought about home, she thought about their new house on Jacaranda Street. Sure, it had ugly, peeling wallpaper and old, rickety ceiling fans instead of central air. But there was plenty of closet space and an old-fashioned tub that was perfect for long bubble baths. And her cat, Emerald, loved its sunny windowsills, ideal for napping and bird-stalking.

Josh's face had frozen on the screen.

"Josh?" Devin said, pressing random keys. "Are you there?"

A moment later, the image stirred to life.

"—class," Josh finished.

"What? I totally missed, like, the last thirty seconds," Devin told him.

"I said, I've got history, then English, then algebra, then lunch with Nina and Cameron and the Goose. And Mrs. Hendrickson's sick, so we have a sub. He doesn't know what he's doing, so he pretty much lets us goof off the whole time. He even lets us text in class," Josh replied. "How 'bout you?"

"How 'bout me what?"

"What classes do you have this morning?" Josh asked.

"Um…uh…the same as last semester, basically," Devin replied. She glanced around the room, trying to find her shirt for cheer practice. Where had she left it? Last fall, when her mom had practically blackmailed her into joining the squad, Devin could have cared less about wearing the "right" clothes for practice. Boys' soccer shorts and ratty old Hanes tees had suited her just fine.

Now things were different. She was the JV cocaptain. She had to do this right. Actually, she *wanted* to do this right.

"Devver? You still there?"

"Sorry, I'm here!"

"Hey, did I tell you I got an A on my epic bio project about acid rain? You know, the one I was forced to do with my new BFF Stephanie von Tresser?"

"That's great!" Devin said distractedly.

"Um, Devver? That was a joke. About Stephanie being my new BFF. You were supposed to laugh," Josh said pointedly. "Because Stephanie is so mean that she makes Darcy Dingman seem like the nicest person on the planet. Get it?"

Devin smiled. She had no idea who Darcy Dingman was.

"*Josh!* You're going to miss your bus!" Devin could hear Mrs. Griffith yell.

Josh sighed. "Oops, gotta go. Skype later?"

"Sure. Have a great day."

"You too, Devver."

The Skype window went dark. Josh was gone. Devin realized that her smile was still plastered to her face.

She also realized that she'd forgotten to apologize to him for last night.

They'd had a dumb fight. It was the whole reason they'd arranged to Skype this morning, actually. Josh had posted his first YouTube video a few days ago, of him playing guitar and singing an original composition. He'd asked her to check it out, and she'd forgotten. He'd reminded her about the post three times before getting totally annoyed and accusing her of not being interested in *his* thing (music) because she was so wrapped up in *her* thing (cheering).

She'd finally taken a look at the video late last night. It was a song called "So Far Away," about two people who used to be in love.

It seemed like a million years ago since Josh had visited her for New Year's. Was it only last week? His visit had been a weird combination of fun and awkward. She'd shown him around Sunny Valley and taken him to Humble Pie, which had the *best* slices—even better than the pizza place they used to go to in Spring Park. They'd gone to the movies three days in a row and gorged on nacho cheese–flavored popcorn and root beer.

Those were the fun parts. As for the awkward stuff… well, if Devin was being totally honest with herself, things hadn't exactly felt romantic during their visit.

New Year's Eve, for example. They'd stayed up to watch the ball drop. At midnight, Mrs. Isle had excused herself to the kitchen to make some hot chocolate, so that Devin and Josh could have a minute alone. Josh had leaned in for the big New Year's kiss… and Devin had leaned in to kiss him… and they'd ended up missing each other's lips. Two seconds later, they'd gone back to sitting on opposite ends of the couch, making fun of the holiday revelers on TV.

Devin liked Josh so much. More than any guy she'd ever met. But lately, their Skype sessions were becoming fewer and farther between. And when they did manage to connect, they didn't have a lot to say. In person, they were more like good friends than girlfriend and boyfriend.

Devin's life was Southern California, Northside High, cheerleading, and her new friends. Josh's life was Northern California, Spring Park High, music, and their old friends.

Would they get back in sync soon? Or were they destined to be on parallel tracks forever?

❇

"IMHO? The only solution to boyfriend problems is to dump the boyfriend," Emily told Devin. "Wow! When-slash-why did Marylou Jenkins get highlights? It looks like a family of skunks is nesting on her head."

Devin giggled and bit into her turkey-on-rye sandwich. It was lunchtime, and she and Emily were sitting together in the sunlit cafeteria. Chloe and Kate normally ate with them, but they had slightly different schedules this semester, and didn't have lunch until next period.

Devin had told Emily about her not-great Skype session with Josh. She wasn't much of a confider, but Emily was so easy to talk to—not to mention totally relentless when it came to extracting personal information.

Taking a sip of root beer, Devin mulled over Emily's advice. "I don't want to break up with Josh. He's special," she said finally.

"Every guy is special in his own way. Like, see Naveen Chanda over there?" Emily pointed with her kombucha-tea bottle. "He has really, really special pecs. And see Malcolm Heller? He's got the most special blue eyes I've ever seen."

Devin grinned. Emily was certifiably boy-crazy.

"What about you? Do you, you know, like anyone?" Devin asked curiously.

Emily picked up her fork and stabbed a cherry tomato

with it. "Nah. I'm *waaay* too busy for guys right now," she said vaguely.

Devin frowned. Was it her imagination, or was Emily hiding something? Did she have a secret crush?

Emily took a sip of her drink and leaned across the table. Devin wasn't sure what kombucha tea was, but it smelled kind of gross, like sour pickles. "Dev, if I tell you something, do you promise you won't tell Chloe and Kate?" Emily said in a low voice.

"Sure," Devin said, flattered. She had always thought of herself as the fourth wheel in the Emily-Chloe-Kate triumvirate—and now Emily was confiding in her? *Cool.*

"Remember Hashtag? The band I sang with at homecoming? They—I mean, we—might get a record deal. Can you believe it?" Emily said excitedly.

"Omigod, for real? That's incredible!" Devin cried out.

"The thing is, they want more songs from us. Which means more work. And if we actually get a contract, well, I'd have to give up cheering," Emily rambled on. "I'll barely have time for school. I'm not sure how my parents would feel about it, either. I mean, it's one thing to sing with Hashtag for fun. It's another thing to do it, you know, like, professionally. I'm only fourteen."

"Yeah, I see your point," Devin said.

"That's why I can't tell Chloe and Kate. Not yet,

anyway. They're *way* too obsessed with cheering. They wouldn't understand."

Devin nodded. "Got it."

"Great!" Emily reached into her backpack and pulled out a glittery spiral notebook labeled REALLY IMPORTANT STUFF in purple marker, with REALLY underlined three times. "Okay, new topic! I have to come up with a killer concept for the fund-raiser on the twenty-fifth. Do you have any brilliant ideas? Say yes!"

"Who me? Um, not really," Devin replied, flustered. She wasn't used to people asking her for fund-raising advice. Back in Spring Park, her gymnastics team had raised money by selling wrapping paper, and she had sold exactly nine dollars' worth: to her dad, her mom, and one of her mom's coworkers at the hospital. Last fall, she'd made a strawberry-rhubarb pie for the cheerleading squad's bake sale. That was the extent of her fund-raising experience.

"Well, you've gotta help me. I'm thinking maybe a car wash. Or a dunking booth. Or—" Emily stopped and shook her head. "No, *boring!* We need something fresh and new so we can rake in a ton of money. Half of it will go to Nationals, and the other half will go to the charity of our choice. Coach Steele told me we still have to raise some money for Nationals expenses, or the cheerleaders and their families will have to cough that up on their own. Which would suck."

Their squad was big into charities and community service in general. Devin liked that. Last fall, they had donated money to a local organization called Hearts Heal. In fact, after practice yesterday, Chloe had mentioned something about doing extra volunteer work for the group on her own.

"I know, let's have a brainstorming sesh!" Emily suggested. "I'll text Chloe and Kate right away. Maybe after practice today. But don't forget, mum's the word about Hashtag." She pulled her phone out of her pocket.

"Emily," Devin warned. "Over there!" The campus guard was standing by the entrance, surveying the cafeteria. His sole purpose in life was to narc on students who violated the school's no-texting-on-campus rule.

Emily slid her phone onto her lap, typing without looking at the screen. "Done! Now, what were we talking about before? Oh, yeah, special boys. Oooh, check it out, there's a *really* special one heading in our direction."

Devin glanced up. A tall, lanky guy with black curls and broad shoulders was walking toward their table. *Yeah, he's definitely cute*, Devin thought.

"Mateo Torres. JV basketball team. Forward," Emily whispered.

"O-kay. Why are we whispering?" Devin asked, confused.

"He probably wants to ask me to the Valentine's Day

dance. Watch and learn, Devin." Emily sat up straight and tossed her hair over her shoulders. "Hey, Mateo," she began in a singsong voice.

Mateo stopped in front of their table. But he wasn't looking at Emily. He was looking at *Devin*.

"Hi, Emily. Hi...Devin, right?" Mateo said with a friendly smile.

"Yeah. Hey." Devin waved awkwardly.

"You're in my history class. I sit two rows over. Were you expecting that pop quiz this morning?" Mateo asked her. "I totally wasn't."

"Me neither," Devin admitted.

"Hey, do you have a partner yet for the mock-trial project? Maybe we could work on it together," Mateo suggested.

Devin blinked. "Um, sure."

"Great! Why don't you give me your number, and I'll text you?"

"Um, sure."

Devin and Mateo traded numbers. Then he waved and took off.

Emily grabbed Devin's arm. "Do. You. Know. What. Just. Happened?" she said breathlessly.

Devin shook her head, dazed.

"You scored the hottest member of the JV basketball team!" Emily exclaimed.

"What? *No!* I didn't score anyone. I have a boyfriend," Devin protested.

"Uh-huh. You keep telling yourself that," Emily said with a wink.

Devin frowned. Then smiled. Then frowned again. Cute guys didn't just come up to her and ask her to do stuff with them. Even if it was only to work on a project for history class.

Guilt washed over her. She shouldn't be happy about receiving attention from another boy.

What would Josh think?

CHAPTER 4

Kate adjusted the white ribbon on her long brown ponytail before spilling out onto the floor with the rest of the squad. It was Friday night, halftime at the JV basketball game, and they were about to run their Nationals routine. It was nearly identical to the routine they'd done at Regionals, which had originally been choreographed by Chloe and Devin. Since then, Coach Steele had hired a professional choreographer to tweak and refine their moves, especially the stunts.

Kate blinked into the blindingly bright lights as she took her position along with the other girls. The Northside crowd roared. Kate loved their custom-made uniforms:

bold blue shell tops and A-line skirts trimmed with white and gold, NORTHSIDE embroidered across their chests in big, loopy cursive.

From somewhere in the bleachers, she heard a distant "Go, Kate!" Who was that?

But there was no time to figure it out. Coach Steele had plugged her iPod into the sound system, and music blasted over the speakers: a superfast pop remix of Carly Rae Jepsen, Lady Gaga, and some other club hits, with special sound effects mixed in to cue the transitions.

"I've got this," Kate whispered to herself. It was the mantra she'd been using to psych herself up before big routines. Unlike Chloe and Emily, Kate didn't find that cheering came naturally, and she wasn't a mad-genius tumbler like Devin, either. The mantra helped shift her brain into super-cheerleader mode.

"I've got this," she repeated.

Chloe looked over her shoulder and nodded twice. It was the signal.

The squad started with toe touch handsprings, and then the front six girls performed tucks. Their sync was a little off, with both Jenn and Arianna putting their hands down during their tucks.

The music switched, and the squad split off into groups for their stunt sequences, with the extra girls spotting and tumbling. Kate was one of the bases in her group, along with Chloe, Jenn, and Marcy; Emily was their top girl. In general, bases had to be strong and able to support the top girls. Top girls had to be good at high-flying acrobatics. No matter what, though, all the squad members had to have total and complete trust in one another so they could hit their stunts.

All the cheerleaders held their arms against their sides and silently counted to the music. Then they hit their full-up extensions while, in the middle, Emily shot up into a liberty, her leg locked tight and her arms straight up in the air. She then reached out her arms to connect with Kalyn and Lexi, and switched from one leg to the other, nailing her tic-tock to complete the pyramid. The two side groups transitioned and tossed their top girls into basket tosses.

Unfortunately, the stunt groups were off-rhythm, and the right side finished its basket toss well before the left side. Kate winced inwardly as everyone struggled to get back in sync. She managed to keep a huge smile plastered to her face, though. One of the most important things she'd learned from Coach Steele was to "keep smiling and keep going" no matter what.

The music stopped. The top girls dismounted into cradles and walked briskly to their spots for the cheer section.

"ALL RIGHT!" Devin and Chloe yelled in unison.

Behind them, signs were raised, leading the fans through the cheer.

"NORTHSIDE FANS…IN THE STANDS…YELL BLUE…AND GOLD!" all the girls cheered. They clapped their hands twice.

"YELL BLUE AND GOLD!" Two more claps.

"Blue and gold!" the crowd yelled.

"COME ON, FANS, GET ON YOUR FEET! LISTEN TO…THE NORTHSIDE BEAT!"

Carley and Lexi were in extensions, leading the crowd with their shiny signs that read BLUE on one side and GOLD on the other. Kate was in the center prep with her poms. She felt nervous; she didn't like being the focus of attention.

I've got this, she repeated in her head. She took a deep breath.

"WE SAY BLUE, YOU SAY GOLD!" Carley and Lexi yelled.

"BLUE!" the girls shouted.

"Blue!" the crowd responded.

"GOLD!" Carley and Lexi flipped their signs over to the GOLD side.

"Gold!"

"WE SAY WOLF PACK, YOU SAY FIGHT." Kate dropped her blue pom when she hit her motion. *That was stupid*, she thought. She should be able to hold on to her poms! Still, she made herself keep smiling.

"WOLF PACK!"

"Fight!" the crowd responded.

"WOLF PACK! FIGHT!" The girls re-formed their lines for the big finish.

The music transitioned and the team sprang into action for the dance sequence. They raised their arms high up in the air and then lowered them to their hips, sliding back and forth. Kate and eight other girls rolled to the mat while the other half of the team remained standing.

As the Timberwolves danced to the pulsing beat, they directed all their attention to the crowd. Cheerleading was first and foremost about revving up the fans.

Then Devin, Arianna, Jenn, and Leila spread out to the four corners of the mat while the other girls completed their dance sequence. A second later, Devin shot across the mat, completing a round-off, back handspring, full.

That girl is so good, Kate thought, gazing in wonder at Devin.

The other tumblers followed suit. Unfortunately, Leila messed up her full. Still, the people in the stands clapped and roared. There was just one more element to go. Following the music switch, the bases lifted the top girls in a heel stretch pyramid. They held the position for eight beats. This time, they were all together. And the crowd went wild!

As the applause continued, Kate and the other girls jogged over to the bench, poms raised high in the air. Just then, Kate noticed Adam Findlay way up in the bleachers. Her heart raced. He must have been the one who'd shouted her name.

Kate and Adam, who was a junior, had met back in September in Mrs. Lawrence's Advanced English class. They had been friends ever since, and a little more than friends since the homecoming dance. Kate blushed, thinking about their first kiss, and all the kisses after that. The two of them were taking it slow, though, even if they didn't always agree on the definition of *slow*. For now, their relationship consisted mostly of talking on the phone, texting, and stealing kisses between classes.

Kate had never liked a boy before she met Adam. She had always been afraid of getting hurt. For one thing, her parents' marriage and divorce had left a bad taste in her mouth. After their split-up, Kate's mom, Vanessa, had moved to New York City to live with her boyfriend, Laurent. All Kate knew of her mother these days came from birthday and Christmas cards and an occasional e-mail.

Kate continued scanning the crowd. Her dad, Andrew, was sitting with Emily's parents and Chloe's parents. There was no sign of Kate's stepmom, Barbara; her stepbrothers, Garrett and Jack; or her little sister, Sasha. Barbara was probably home, putting them to bed.

Kate joined Emily and Chloe on the bench and reached

for a Gatorade. Devin plopped down on the other side of Chloe and wiped her brow with a towel.

Before any of them could say a word, Leila strolled over, narrowing her kohl-lined eyes at Chloe and Devin. Her friend Marcy was at her heels. "Way to lead, *captains*," Leila said sarcastically. "That. Sucked."

"Excuse me?" Chloe snapped. Devin crossed her arms defensively.

"Thanks for the constructive criticism, Leila. It's really helpful, coming from someone who tanked her full," Emily sniped.

"What are you talking about? Leila's full was increds!" Marcy spoke up. Marcy's nickname was Savett's Shadow because she followed Leila around like a loyal puppy.

Coach Steele strode over to the bench, interrupting their squabble. Her face was a stony mask. "Listen up, ladies. I know this is the first time we've done our routine full out since Regionals," she began. "It was a good try, but needless to say, we've still got a *lot* of work to do between now and February eighth."

"I totally blame our leadership," Leila stage-whispered to Marcy. "If we'd elected better captains last September, we wouldn't have these problems."

"Totally," Marcy said, her head bobbing.

"Excuse me, Savett and Martinez? Unless the gym is on fire, please keep your mouths zipped shut and listen up,"

Coach Steele said sternly. "Anyway... fortunately for us, I just cleared our weekend practice schedule with Principal Cilento. We start this Sunday. Two PM. Attendance is mandatory. And nonnegotiable." She glanced at her watch. "Okay, let's get back on the floor. Halftime's almost over."

Kate noticed that Emily's face had gone white. "What's the matter?" Kate whispered.

"Nothing. Nothing's the matter. Everything's fine," her friend replied quickly.

Kate saw Emily shoot a panicked look at Devin. Devin smiled sympathetically. *What does Devin know about Emily that Chloe and I don't?* Kate wondered.

After the game, Adam came up to Kate in the hallway outside the gym. With his scruffy black hair and horn-rimmed glasses, he looked both geeky and adorable. She waved, happy to see him.

"Hey, Cheer Girl!" Adam said, stepping forward to hug her.

"Uniform!" Kate cried out. One of Coach Steele's hard-and-fast rules was no physical contact with boys while in uniform, including hand-holding, hugging, and kissing.

Adam crossed his arms over his chest and stepped back quickly. "Forgot. Sorry," he apologized.

"It's okay. Thanks for coming to the game," Kate told him shyly.

"Of course. You were awesome," Adam complimented her.

"I made a couple of mistakes, actually," Kate admitted.

"No way. You were perfect. Better than perfect. I'm going to write a Shakespearean sonnet about that killer move you made—you know, the, uh, twirly, jumpy one," Adam told her.

Adam pretended not to know anything about cheering, even though he could execute a perfect standing back tuck. In fact, when he and Kate first met, he had made some pretty disparaging comments about cheerleading. But he'd come around quickly, especially after Kate had called him out on his unfair stereotypes, like how cheerleaders were dumb and shallow. Among other things, she loved to tease him about the fact that she'd already taken her PSATs, as a freshman, and that she'd scored higher than he had.

Kate noticed three guys hovering behind Adam.

"Dude, aren't you going to introduce us?" one of them said.

Adam turned. "Oh! Yeah, sorry. This is my...um... this is Kate. Kate, these are my friends Jason, Tucker, and Chen."

Kate reached up to smooth her hair. Did she look okay?

Was she a sweaty mess? She was a bundle of nerves all of a sudden. She'd never met Adam's friends before.

"Hey," Tucker said with a wave.

"So you're the new girlfriend," Chen stated bluntly.

Kate startled. "I'm not—"

"She's not—" Adam said at the same time.

"Don't forget about me, you jerk." A girl stepped forward and slid her hand through Adam's arm.

Adam grinned at her. "Sorry. Kate, this is Willow. Willow's my annoying neighbor," he joked.

"Not as annoying as you, nerd," Willow teased back.

"Hi, Willow." Kate tried not to stare at Willow's hand tucked cozily in Adam's elbow—or to notice how pretty Willow was. With her waist-length auburn hair, big blue eyes, and chunky black glasses, she was the perfect storm of sexy and smart.

"Soooo... Kate, right? You're only in ninth grade, huh? Finland here usually goes for older girls," Willow said with a wink.

"Ha-ha," Adam said drily.

"Finland?" Kate managed feebly.

"Nickname. It's a play on Findlay, in case it wasn't obvious," Adam explained to Kate.

Chen jangled his car keys. "We're heading out. You still need a ride?" he asked Adam.

"Oh, yeah." Adam extracted himself from Willow. He

leaned forward to kiss Kate on the cheek, then pulled back when she shot him a warning look. "Sorry. I keep forgetting about the uniform thing. Wouldn't want your coach to lock you up in her dungeon, right? I'll text you later."

"Sure." Kate forced herself to smile.

Adam gave her a salute, then turned and walked down the hall with his friends. Including Willow. Kate stood there staring after them, her stomach in knots.

It was so unfair. Coach Steele's no-physical-contact rule meant that Kate couldn't let Adam hug her or even peck her on the cheek, while Willow could put her hands all over him.

Kate took the coach's rules very seriously. Maybe *too* seriously. In fact, she lived in constant, paranoid fear of accruing demerits and getting kicked off the team.

"Hey, Kate!" Chloe bounded up to her, sipping from a water bottle. "You were awesome tonight. Your tumbling pass was amazing!"

"Thanks," Kate said distractedly.

"I know we have a lot of work to do still, as a team. But I'm certain we'll get there before Nationals," Chloe added, with her usual optimism.

"Uh-huh." Kate watched as Willow reached over and ruffled Adam's hair. *Seriously?*

Chloe followed Kate's gaze. "That's Adam, right? And his friends? I guess you're like one of the juniors now. Are you going to forget about us little people?" she teased.

"Yes. I mean, no. I mean . . . who is she, anyway?"

"Who's who?" Chloe asked, puzzled.

"That girl, Willow. She acts like she owns Adam or something."

"Why, what did she do?"

Kate shrugged. "I don't know. She's constantly touching him in this flirty, obnoxious way."

Chloe wrapped her arm around her friend's shoulder. "You know what? I'm sure it's not personal. Maybe she's one of those boy-crazy girls. Like an evil version of Emily."

Kate grinned.

"I wouldn't worry about her. Adam likes *you*," Chloe told her.

"You're right," Kate said. But inside, she wasn't so sure.

She had a mantra to boost her confidence as a cheerleader. Now she just needed a mantra to boost her confidence with boys.

CHAPTER 5

The next day, Chloe slid out of the front seat of her mother's Mercedes and stepped onto the sidewalk. She hoisted her backpack over her shoulders and looked around, trying to get her bearings. She'd never been in this part of Sunny Valley before.

"Everything okay?" her mother, Joanie Davis, called out from inside the car.

"Yes. Can you come back for me in a couple of hours? Like, two, two fifteen?" Chloe asked.

"I have my massage appointment at one thirty, so your father will pick you up. He's playing golf with some of the other lawyers from his office, but he should be done by then. Have fun!" Mrs. Davis fluttered her hand, with her perfectly French-manicured fingernails, at Chloe.

While her mother waited in the car, Chloe walked up to the gray one-story building before her. A simple sign above the doorway said:

HEARTS HEAL
EVERYONE WELCOME

Hearts Heal was one of the many charities in town that the Northside cheer squad had raised money for in the past. The nonprofit organization helped low-income and other economically challenged families. Among other things, Hearts Heal ran a food pantry, mentored kids, and helped people find jobs.

Over break, Chloe had thought about volunteering for the organization. Sure, she already performed community service as part of her team commitment. But it was important to go above and beyond. She came from a wealthy family who took ski trips to Aspen and drove fancy cars. But not everyone was so fortunate, and she wanted to do something to make a difference. It was a value that cheerleading had instilled in her.

So she'd e-mailed Hearts Heal just after Christmas, and someone at the office had e-mailed back and asked if she wanted to help out on Saturday afternoons. Of course, she didn't exactly have a lot of spare time on her hands these days, especially with Nationals coming up, and now with extra practices on Sundays. But she could spare a couple of hours a week for a good cause—couldn't she?

Humming "Your Heart Is a Muscle" and swaying her shoulders to the beat, Chloe strode up to the glass door and opened it...

...and stopped in her tracks.

The inside of Hearts Heal was a total zoo. Dozens of people sifted through crowded racks of clothes and discarded items on the floor. Nearby, at the front of a long line, a man complained to a young woman about paperwork. Babies cried. Phones rang. Parents chased after their children.

"Hello. Welcome. How can we help you today?"

Chloe turned. A petite silver-haired woman smiled kindly at her.

"Oh! I'm not... that is, I'm here to be a volunteer. They told me to arrive at twelve," Chloe explained.

"You must be Chloe Davis, then. I'm Mrs. Hillman. I'm in charge of the volunteers."

"It's nice to meet you, Mrs. Hillman."

"Come this way, and I'll get you set up. As you can see, we're very busy. With the economy the way it is, there are a number of families who need our services. I'm very glad you're here," Mrs. Hillman told her.

"Me too," Chloe said, meaning it.

Chloe followed Mrs. Hillman to an adjoining room piled high with boxes and plastic bags. A tall, lanky guy sat cross-legged on the floor, plugged into an iPod as he organized piles of clothes. He had wavy, dark red hair and looked kind of familiar.

When he saw Chloe and Mrs. Hillman, he removed his earbuds and smiled. "Hey. Mrs. Hillman, do you need me for something?"

"Yes, Daniel. I wanted to introduce you to our new volunteer, Chloe Davis," Mrs. Hillman said. "Chloe, this is Daniel Moore. Daniel's been one of our most dependable volunteers since I can remember." She added, "Daniel, can I leave Chloe with you? I thought you could get her up to speed on our sorting procedures."

"No problem," Daniel said.

Mrs. Hillman left to answer a call. Daniel turned to Chloe. "Okay. Basically, this is how it works. People in the community donate used clothing and shoes. Drop-off is Saturday morning. You and I are going to go through the donations and sort them into a bunch of categories."

Chloe nodded. "Got it. What are the categories?"

"Well, first we sort into tops, bottoms, suits, dresses, pj's, coats, shoes, and miscellaneous," Daniel rattled off. "Miscellaneous can be scarves, mittens, things like that. Then we sort into men's, women's, children's, and babies'. After that, we sort into sizes. Sizes can be kinda tricky, so ask me if you get confused. And, by the way, all this stuff's supposed to be clean, ironed, and ready to go. But if it's not, put it in that container over there." Daniel pointed to a blue plastic bin with a handwritten sign on it that said LAUNDRY.

"Okay."

The two of them got to work. Chloe quickly fell into the rhythm of the task. As she folded a pair of size five acid-washed jeans, she thought about all the outfits she had in her closet, most of which she never wore anymore. She made a mental note to gather them up and bring them in soon.

"So how long have you been a volunteer here?" she asked Daniel.

"Like a year, year and a half? My high school actually requires community service. Although I'd want to do this even if it wasn't required. HH does really important work for the community," Daniel replied.

"What high school do you go to?" Chloe asked curiously.

"Sunny Valley Performing Arts. Can't you tell?" Daniel grinned and pointed at his T-shirt, which had a picture of a stringed instrument on it.

Chloe peered at the image. "You play the violin?" she guessed.

"Yep. Classical." Daniel balled up a UCLA hoodie and tossed it into the laundry bin. "Score! Yeah, my parents claim that when I was four years old, I made a quote-unquote violin out of rubber bands and an empty Kleenex box and played it constantly. Eventually, they saved up enough money to buy me a real one, and lessons, too."

"That's so cool!" Chloe mostly hung out with cheerleaders and jocks. Besides Emily and the Hashtag members, she didn't know any musicians. And she definitely didn't know any *classical* musicians. "Do you like it there? At Sunny Valley Performing Arts, I mean?"

"Yes. And no. I have a regular tenth-grade curriculum in the morning, like advanced algebra and bio and whatever. Then I have music all afternoon—private lessons, chamber, orchestra, ear training, theory, you name it." Daniel paused to hold up a pair of worn leather gloves to the light. "It's pretty intense. But I want to be a professional violinist. And Performing Arts is the best place to train for that."

Chloe nodded. She admired a guy who was passionate about what he did. She felt the same way about cheering. In fact, she'd been thinking a lot about her future lately. Over break, she'd even checked out some websites for colleges with strong cheering programs. Not that she had to worry about college applications yet, but still...

"What about you? Do you go to one of the public

high schools? Or St. Dominic? Or the Academy?" Daniel asked her.

"Northside High. I'm a freshman. I totally love it," Chloe replied.

"My little sister goes there, too. Although…" Daniel hesitated. "I'm not sure how much longer we'll be living in Sunny Valley. We may be moving. I don't know."

Chloe turned toward him. "Wait, what? You're moving? But what about school and violin and all that stuff?"

"Yeah. The thing is, our dad got laid off from his job a few months ago," Daniel explained. "My parents don't like to talk about it, but my sister and I overheard them last week, worrying about money. We might have to sell our house. And if that happens, I'm not sure where we'll go. Maybe move to Albuquerque and live with my grandparents or something."

"Oh my gosh! That's awful!" Chloe exclaimed.

"Sorry if I'm oversharing. I figured I should let you know, since I may not be volunteering here for much longer. Albuquerque's kind of far away." Daniel smiled sadly.

"No, no! Don't be sorry!" Chloe told him.

The door opened and Mrs. Hillman stuck her head inside. "Daniel? Your mom and sister are here to pick you up," she called out.

"Thanks, Mrs. Hillman." Daniel stood and brushed his

hands against his jeans. He picked up his iPod and stuffed it into his back pocket. "Sorry to cut out on you early, Chloe. I'm usually here till two, but I have this audition I can't miss."

"No problem! I can finish up," Chloe replied.

"See you next Saturday. Now you know my whole life story, and I totally want to hear yours," Daniel told her.

He waved and left. As he walked through the door, Chloe noticed a woman and a girl waiting for him on the other side. Their backs were turned to Chloe.

The girl had long, wavy hair the same color as Daniel's. Chloe scooted up to the door before it closed and held it open a crack.

She stifled a gasp when she caught sight of the girl's profile.

It was Gemma Moore from cheerleading.

Gemma was Daniel's little sister!

CHAPTER 6

"Los Angeles is sick. Everything happens here. Sunny Valley is totally boring in comparison," Travis remarked to Emily as he turned his car onto Melrose Avenue.

"Definitely," Emily agreed. She put her feet up on the dashboard, rolled down the window, and gazed out at the row of trendy restaurants, cafés, and boutiques that lined the famous street. "Omigosh, is that Harry Styles walking into that hair salon?" she practically screamed.

"Um, no? If it was, there'd be paparazzi all over the place," Travis told her. "I wouldn't be surprised if he's somewhere in LA, though. This city is crawling with celebrities."

Emily nodded mutely. *Pinch me,* she wanted to say. *I'm driving around in Hollywood—and omigosh there's that famous gym I read about—on my way to meet some VIP at Rampage Records!*

If only she could share all this with Chloe and Kate. But they would freak out and tell her she was making a huge mistake, especially with Nationals coming up. Last November, Emily had almost made the team forfeit Regionals because she'd been recording with Hashtag at SV Studios and barely got to the competition on time. And her friends wouldn't appreciate the fact that she'd lied about missing the mandatory Sunday practice session today. She'd texted them both earlier, saying she had the flu.

She'd lied to her parents, too, telling them that Travis was giving her a ride to a one o'clock Hashtag rehearsal at his house, followed by the two o'clock practice at school. They had no idea she was in Los Angeles right now, en route to a two-thirty meeting at a record company.

They would totally kill me if they found out, Emily thought with a shudder. But she couldn't dwell on that. She had to focus on the here and now. Was she wearing the right outfit? (It had taken hours to decide between her black-jeans-and-blazer combo and her floral sundress before finally settling on the former. She'd even added eye shadow, blush, and lip gloss, which she normally didn't wear.) What should she say at the meeting? Or should she let Travis do all the talking?

Ten minutes later, Travis pulled into the parking lot of a modern white building on Santa Monica Boulevard. Once inside, they rode the elevator up to the third floor.

"You look pretty, Ems," Travis complimented her. "You're wearing, like...lip stuff."

Emily tried to think of a funny comeback. Usually, she was full of them. But at the moment, with Travis staring at her in a dreamy-crush way, she felt completely tongue-tied. "Thanks" was all she could manage.

The elevator doors opened to reveal a glass-walled lobby with a panoramic view of the city. Dozens of vinyl album covers and framed music awards covered the bright orange walls. The receptionist asked them to have a seat while she called Jacinta.

A cute guy with spiky platinum hair came out shortly and introduced himself as Niles, Jacinta's assistant. "I'll take you back to Jacinta now. Can I get you guys something? Water? A latte? Green tea?"

"A glass of water, please," Travis said as he and Emily followed Niles down the hall.

"I'll have the same," Emily said.

"Ice or room temp?"

"Um...ice?" Emily said.

Travis nodded.

"I'll get that for you straightaway." Niles paused in front of a doorway at the end of the hall and waved them in.

A tall woman with long, shiny black hair rose from her desk and held out her hand. "Travis. Emily. I'm Jacinta. Welcome! Thanks so much for giving up your Sunday afternoon to come see me," she said warmly.

"Do you guys always work weekends?" Travis asked as he shook Jacinta's hand.

"Not always. But this time of year, with the Grammys coming up, we're insanely busy. Plus, we're launching Calla's new single this week," Jacinta explained.

"Calla's got a new single?" Emily burst out.

Jacinta smiled. "You're a fan? I'll have Niles send you a download."

"Seriously? Thank you!" Emily gushed.

Jacinta gestured for Emily and Travis to make themselves comfortable on a white leather couch. Jacinta sat in a chair across from them. Niles came in with two glasses of ice water and set them down on the surfboard-shaped coffee table.

Emily took a long sip of her water. It had mint sprigs and lemon slices in it. *Even the water's fancy here*, she thought in awe.

"So here's the deal," Jacinta began. "We absolutely

loved your demo. Hashtag has a raw, passionate hometown vibe that we think will resonate with today's audience." She paused and steepled her hands under her chin. "We'd love for you to write and record a few softer, slower numbers, though. Maybe a couple of love songs featuring your vocals, Emily?"

"Me?" Emily said, surprised.

Travis regarded her with a pleased I-told-you-so expression.

"Yes, you. You have a terrific voice," Jacinta said enthusiastically. "Plus, you know when to be a diva with the vocals and when to take a backseat and let the instrumentals dominate. Not every fourteen-year-old has those kinds of instincts. You're a natural performer, Emily."

"Um...thanks!" Emily said, blushing. She couldn't wait to text Chloe, Kate, and Devin and repeat everything Jacinta had just said.

Except...Devin was the only one she could tell. Chloe and Kate thought she was laid up in bed with the flu. *Ugh.*

Jacinta picked up her phone and scrolled through it. "Just checking our schedule here. Hmmm. Why don't we set Hashtag up in the recording studio in, say...mid-February? How about February sixteenth? That would give you a little over a month to write a couple new songs, rehearse, and so forth. We'll also have time to talk to your parents by then, too, since we'll need to have them on board. What do you say?"

February sixteenth? Emily gulped. Nationals were on the eighth and ninth. They wouldn't even be flying back from Orlando until the tenth. Emily planned to shift into high gear as soon as they were back to get ready for the Valentine's Day dance; it was set for the fifteenth, since there was a basketball game on the fourteenth.

All of which left *zero* time for Emily to get ready for a recording session.

"I'm not sure if—" Emily began.

"February sixteenth is perfect!" Travis cut in with a quick sideways glance at Emily. "We're really psyched about your interest in Hashtag. We won't let you down, Ms. Cruz."

"Jacinta, please." Her phone buzzed. "I'm so sorry, I have to take this. There's a fashion show tonight to raise money for charity, and one of our artists is a runway model. I think she's having a little emergency."

Emily perked up. For a brief second, she forgot all about her scheduling nightmare.

A fashion show? For charity?

Why hadn't *she* thought of that?

As soon as Emily got into Travis's car, she extracted Chad from her purse. Her fingers practically flew as she texted Devin with an update:

Just got out of Rampage Records meeting. So much 2 tell U!!!

A minute. Two minutes. Three minutes. No reply.

Then Emily remembered. It was the middle of the afternoon. Devin was at Northside High with the rest of the squad, practicing. For a moment, Emily pictured the seventeen girls stretching on the mats, doing toe touches, running tumbling passes—all without her. She bit her lip, trying not to feel like a jerk.

"So this is epic, right?" Travis was gripping the steering wheel in excitement as he pulled out of the parking lot. He stopped briefly to pop the Hashtag demo into his CD player, then kept driving. "Alex, Kyle, and I can get busy on the new songs. I'd love your help on the lyrics, though. Have you ever written lyrics before?"

"No," Emily replied. "I wrote a poem for English once, about unicorns. But that probably doesn't count, right?"

Travis laughed. "Uh, not exactly what I had in mind. But no worries. I'm sure you'll be a natural at it. Do you want to come over tonight and we can work on it?"

"Um..." Emily hesitated.

Travis glanced over. "Emily? Is there a problem?"

"I'm thinking. About Jacinta's offer, I mean."

"Seriously? Jacinta's giving us the chance to become famous. What's there to think about?"

Emily sighed. Her gaze fell on the Rampage Records tote bag at her feet. Niles had given one to her and one to Travis, filled with Rampage Records coffee mugs, Rampage Records T-shirts, and a pair of Rampage Records sunglasses with the rhinestone initials *RR* on the rims.

She honestly didn't know what to do. Travis was right. Forget the bad timing. Jacinta was handing Emily the opportunity of a lifetime on a silver platter.

There was no question that Emily loved to sing. Or, more accurately, to be up onstage. Last fall, Emily had performed with Hashtag for the Northside homecoming dance. As soon as the night was over, she'd immediately craved more—more blazing spotlights, more cheering crowd, more swaying to the beat with her eyes closed as her voice rose up from a deep, soulful place within her that she'd never known existed.

But she loved being a cheerleader, too. It was a different kind of performing, and it challenged her mentally *and* physically, pushed her to the edge. She had dreamed of being on the NHS JV squad since she was a little kid. She had achieved that dream—and she had a good chance at making the Varsity squad, too, after tryouts in April. Why would she throw all that away?

Emily had signed on to cheer this season and at Nationals. And she was already slacking off. She'd skipped practice today and lied about it to Coach Steele, her parents, and her friends.

As for the recording session on February sixteenth... how on earth was she going to manage that without having to clone herself?

"Well?" Travis prompted her. "What's your decision?"

The second track came on. Travis turned up the volume. Emily listened to herself singing a song about having it all. She sounded good. *Great*, actually.

"Just give me a little time. A few more days. I promise," Emily said finally.

Travis reached over and squeezed her hand. "I understand. Take all the time you need."

"Really?"

"Really."

Emily squeezed his hand back, pleased and surprised that Travis was being so understanding about it all. She started to pull her hand away. But Travis wouldn't let go.

"I know you'll make the right decision in the end," he said, weaving his fingers through hers.

Emily tensed. Was he holding her hand? Were they

holding hands? *What was happening here?* She stared straight ahead and tried to act cool, like it was no big deal, even though her heart was racing wildly in her chest.

They stayed that way all the way home, driving the 101 to Sunny Valley, listening to Hashtag songs full blast.

CHAPTER 7

"So I think you should play the role of the lead defense attorney, and I'll play the second chair," Mateo suggested to Devin.

Devin picked up her pencil and doodled a smiley face in her notebook. "Why do you get the easy part? Not fair," she complained.

"Okay, then *you* play the second chair," Mateo said. "But I think you'd be better with the judge and the jury. The way you talk in class? You have this calm, cool way of convincing Mr. Weaver you're right, even when you're wrong."

"That's because I'm always right," Devin joked.

"Yeah, you wish!" Mateo grinned.

Devin grinned back, wondering for the tenth time why Mateo had asked her to partner up with him for the mock-trial project for history. Was he just a dumb, cute jock who wanted to coast on her straight As in Mr. Weaver's class?

But sitting here, talking to Mateo during Monday afternoon study hall, she was beginning to think that he was anything *but* dumb. Cute, yes. Dumb, not at all. In fact, he'd spent the last half hour explaining to her why it was important that they cite case law during their pre-trial motion. He'd then explained to her what case law and pretrial motions were, since she wasn't familiar with the terms.

Devin had never done a mock trial before; it involved a bunch of people acting out a historical or made-up trial. In this case, Mr. Weaver had assigned them the latter, about a man who'd been arrested for treason. Devin and Mateo were the defense team. The remaining students filled out the rest of the cast, including the prosecution's team, the judge, and the twelve members of the jury. Mr. Weaver planned to play the defendant, a fictional character named Arnold Benedict.

Devin leaned over her notebook, letting her hair spill across the pages. She was glad she'd used her new shampoo, which smelled like strawberries. She idly added black curls to her smiley face. "So how are we going to prove

Mr. Weaver, I mean, Mr. Benedict, innocent?" she wondered out loud.

"We have to sift through the evidence first. Mr. Weaver gave me the file. Here's half of it. I'll take the other half." Mateo handed her a stack of papers.

Devin took the pile from him and began leafing through the pages. "How do you know so much about legal stuff, anyway?" she asked curiously.

"My dad's an immigration lawyer," Mateo replied. "His dad, my *abuelo*, teaches human rights law at UCLA. I think everyone kind of expects me to go to law school someday, too."

"Do *you* want to go to law school?"

"No idea. When I was little, I wanted to be a firefighter, then an astronaut, then a farmer. Oh, and the president of the United States." Mateo smiled. "That's about as far as I've gotten with my career goals."

Devin laughed. "When I was little, I wanted to be a mermaid."

"You would make an awesome mermaid," Mateo told her.

"Gosh, thanks!"

"You're welcome. Speaking of, have you ever gone scuba diving? I just got my certification."

"No, but that's so cool!" Devin had always admired divers. She herself had a hard time even putting her head underwater. *So much for being a mermaid,* she thought wryly.

"So what do your parents do?" Mateo asked.

"My mom's a nurse, and my dad teaches computer science at UCSF," Devin replied.

"UCSF—as in...San Francisco? That's kind of far away, isn't it?"

"My parents are divorced. My mom and I just moved down here last summer. She works at Sunny Valley County Hospital," Devin explained.

Mateo raised his eyebrows. "Wow. I didn't know. My parents are divorced, too."

Devin startled. "Oh! I'm sorry."

"Yeah, me too. Do your parents still talk to each other?"

Devin shook her head. "Almost never. They had a really, really bad breakup. My mom totally wanted to work things out, and my dad totally didn't."

"Same here. We live with my mom—my little brother, Sammy, and me, I mean. My older brother, Leo, is a sophomore at USC. Sammy and I have this strict visitation schedule for when my dad can have us on weekends and so forth. But if my mom needs to know where to drop us off or whatever, she won't call him or even text him. She makes me or Sammy do it. And the same with my dad. It's like they're strangers or something."

"That's awful!"

"Yeah. I think adults can be more immature than kids sometimes," Mateo observed sadly.

Devin stared at Mateo. He was so smart. And nice. And sensitive. Boys weren't always the best at sharing their feelings. Mateo seemed to have no problem in that department. In fact, it occurred to her that this was the first time she'd been able to talk—*really* talk—about her parents' divorce with another person. All she ever discussed with Josh was music, movies, their mutual friends at Spring Park, and whether thin-crust, New York–style pizza was better than Chicago-style deep-dish.

As for Emily, Kate, and Chloe...she was slowly becoming better friends with them. But it was definitely a process.

The bell rang. There was a loud, collective scraping of chairs as students scooped up their books and backpacks and headed for the exit.

Devin rose, too—and accidentally dropped her notebook. She bent down to pick it up at the exact same moment Mateo reached for it. Their arms brushed.

"Thanks." Blushing furiously, Devin stood up and clutched her notebook to her chest. For some reason, she couldn't meet Mateo's eyes.

"You're welcome. Where are you off to next?" Mateo asked her.

"Algebra, then English, then cheer practice. How about you?"

"French, then bio, then basketball." Mateo slung his backpack over his shoulder. "Hey...you'll be at the Medham game on Friday, right? Do you want to get together after and maybe grab a burger or something?"

Devin wanted to say yes. Then she remembered that she had a boyfriend. Girls with boyfriends didn't go out for burgers with other guys.

"I...um...that is, I already have plans," she fibbed. "Maybe another time?"

"Sure." Mateo smiled. If he was disappointed, Devin couldn't tell. "Don't forget about the evidence file, okay? Maybe we could go over it on Wednesday during study hall?"

"Sounds like a plan."

Devin said good-bye and rushed off to her algebra class. Out in the hallway, she felt her phone vibrating in her pocket.

She glanced around to make sure the hall monitor wasn't watching, then sneaked a peek at the screen. It was a text from Josh:

Hey, Devver. Miss you. xoxoxo

Devin quickly stuffed the phone back in her pocket, cringing with guilt.

But I didn't do anything, she told herself. *I'm not cheating on Josh.*

So why did she feel as though she was?

      ❋

"Am I overreacting, or was practice, like, a million times harder than usual today?" Emily complained as she, Devin, Chloe, and Kate headed out to the parking lot together. "I swear, my legs feel like nachos that have been nuked too long in the microwave."

"Ew, Emily! My dad's making nachos for dinner tonight." Kate groaned.

"We were awesome, though. It's the first time since Regionals that we all stuck our back handsprings in the closing sequence," Devin pointed out. She'd been working on her cocaptaining skills lately, intent on being more upbeat and making note of her teammates' achievements. "And Chloe...you killed that tumbling pass!"

"Thanks, Devin. Your tumbling pass was amazing, too." Chloe turned to Emily. "I bet you're extra-tired because of yesterday," she remarked.

Emily frowned. "Yesterday? Huh?"

"You know. Because you were sick?" Chloe reminded her.

"Oh, right! Yes. I was sick. Really, really sick. With

the flu. The twenty-four-hour kind, not that longer-than-twenty-four-hour kind. So I'm all better now." Emily gave a little cough. "Well, almost all better."

Devin gave Emily a warning look, wishing that her friend would shut up already. Devin was no expert at lying, but it was probably better to keep one's cover story short and sweet, not long, rambling, and crazy-sounding.

Emily smiled brightly. "So, enough about me and my boring twenty-four-hour flu! I came up with *the* best new idea for our fund-raiser."

"What about our ideas from last week?" Devin asked. The four girls had met at Emily's house last Tuesday for a brainstorming session. It had been more of a popcorn-and-gossip session, but they *had* generated a few good ideas. Devin had liked one of Chloe's suggestions, about decorating coffee cans and distributing them to restaurants and stores around town so that customers could donate their spare change.

"No, this is waaay better. Get this—we're going to do a fashion show!" Emily announced.

"A fashion show?" Devin repeated.

"Yes! I've been thinking about it, and I made up a list of things we'd need to do." Emily stopped on the sidewalk, reached into her backpack, and pulled out her REALLY IMPORTANT STUFF notebook. She flipped to the first page. "So this is the plan. We ask all the cool boutiques in town to each donate one outfit. We install a runway in the gym, like the ones they have at Fashion Week in LA. The audience bids on the outfits. And if you win an outfit, you take it home. If you need a different size, the store will exchange it for you."

"That's . . . kind of genius, actually," Chloe said slowly. "I like it!"

"Who's going to model the clothes?" Kate asked.

"We are! The cheerleaders, I mean. Some of us can be on modeling duty. The rest of us can work the event, do backstage, hair and makeup, whatever." Emily turned to Devin. "What do you think?"

For a brief second, Devin imagined herself strutting down the runway in a stylish outfit—something other than her usual jeans-and-hoodie combo. Would Mateo be there?

Why am I thinking about Mateo? Devin chided herself. *Josh. Think about Josh.*

Emily elbowed her. "Um, earth to Devin? Are you day-dreaming about your boyfriend? Or are you daydreaming about your *other*—"

"*Fashion show!* Yes, count me in!" Devin practically shouted.

"Daydreaming about who?" Chloe asked, glancing between Emily and Devin.

Devin laughed feebly, then changed the subject. "So who's the money going to? I mean, we're raising part of the money for Nationals and the rest of it for our new charity, right?" she added.

"Yeah. Our team needs to decide on a charity." Emily extracted a pen from her pocket and scribbled something in her notebook.

"Actually, I have an idea," Chloe said, raising her hand. "It's kind of related to my new volunteer job."

"You mean Hearts Heal? How did it go on Saturday, by the way?" Kate asked her.

"Amazing! I met this really nice guy there," Chloe replied.

Emily stopped scribbling. "Wait, *what*? Why is this the first time we're hearing about this?" she demanded.

"No, it's not like that," Chloe said quickly. "He's Gemma Moore's brother, Daniel. He's a sophomore at Sunny Valley Performing Arts. He plays the violin."

"Oooh, violin! Sounds super-romantic," Emily teased her.

"Seriously, stop it! He's just a friend!" Chloe insisted.

"Is he cute?" Emily persisted.

"I don't know. I guess?" Chloe blushed. "But back on topic. I have this idea for the charity."

"What is it?" Devin asked.

"I, um, can't say right now. I have to talk to Coach first. But I'll let you guys know ASAP." Chloe glanced over her shoulder. "Oh, hey! *Gemma!*"

Chloe rushed away to catch up to Gemma, who was walking to the parking lot. The two girls starting talking, their heads bent close.

"What was *that* about?" Kate wondered out loud.

"Dunno. Maybe she wanted to talk to Gemma about her hunky brother, Daniel," Emily suggested.

Devin rolled her eyes. Did Emily ever stop thinking about boys?

On the other hand, Devin herself was thinking about boys a lot lately.

One boy in particular, anyway.

What was wrong with her?

CHAPTER 8

"So I was thinking I would do my paper on the theme of isolation in *Othello*," Adam said to Kate. "Unless that's a lame idea. Do you think that's a lame idea?"

"I think it's a *great* idea," Kate told him, tapping her pen against her notebook. "You can work in the stuff about the island of Cyprus—you know, how Iago tries to drive Othello crazy once they are isolated there."

"Yes, totally. That's so smart. But I would have expected no less from you, Lady Kate," Adam said with a smile.

He squeezed her hand, then began typing notes into his iPad. Kate smiled and picked up her decaf latte. The two of them were hanging out at the Mighty Cup in downtown Sunny Valley. She'd never been to the trendy café before, which seemed really crowded for a Monday night, filled mostly with college students and professor types. Kate, Chloe, Emily, and Devin usually went to the fro-yo place down the street. But Adam had suggested it, and she was happy to try something new.

As Adam continued typing, Kate thought about the first time he'd asked her out. In English class he'd given her a tiny, rolled-up scroll adorned with a blue-and-silver twist tie. It contained a quote from Shakespeare's play *Macbeth*, along with a poem he'd written himself, inviting her to the homecoming dance.

Kate smiled at the memory as she took a sip of her latte. Her smile disappeared. The drink was way too bitter for her. Why had she ordered it? Just because Adam had ordered it, too? She should have stuck to something familiar, like hot chocolate or peppermint tea. She glanced over at Emily's brother Eddie, who was working behind the counter. Maybe she should ask him to make her a new drink?

Her phone buzzed. It was a text from Emily:

What R U doing? Can U come by for fashion show sesh in 20?

Kate texted back:

Sorry, can't. @ Mighty Cup with Adam. BTW your
brother's working tonite!

Emily wrote:

Tell him 2 bring home some free cupcakes after his
shift! ☺

"Hey, Finland! Fancy meeting you here!"

Kate's head jerked up at the sound of the familiar,
unwelcome voice. Willow strolled up to their table, wearing skin-tight jeans and a low-cut black T-shirt. Her only
makeup, not that she needed any, was a slash of bright red
lipstick.

Willow sidled up to Adam and kissed him on the cheek.
She smiled coldly at Kate. "Hey... Kim, right?"

Kate felt her entire body tense up. "Actually, my
name is—"

"Wassup, bro?" Jason came over to their table and pretended to knock down Adam's chair. Tucker and Chen followed behind, laughing loudly.

"Dude, stop!" Adam said, chuckling and grabbing
Jason's arm. "What are you guys doing here? Jase, you reek
of garlic."

"Dinner at Humble Pie, remember? We texted you," Chen told him.

"Sorry. Kate and I had to go over our topics for our English papers," Adam apologized.

Willow pulled a chair from the next table and squeezed in between Adam and Kate. "So, Kate. Explain. How did you get into Advanced English for upperclassmen? Are cheerleaders allowed in honors classes?" she asked sweetly.

"*Excuse* me?" Kate snapped.

"Don't mind Willow. She's nice once you get to know her, I promise," Adam told Kate. "And, um...news flash, Wills: Kate happens to be smarter than you and me put together. In fact, she's the only one in Mrs. Lawrence's class who got an A plus on the midterm."

"I don't think *anyone* can be smarter than you, Adam. Well, except for me, maybe," Willow said, snaking her arm around Adam's shoulder. "Remember when we cowrote that epic essay on existential philosophy for Mr. Levy's class? And he loved it so much he wanted to publish it on his blog?"

"Oh, yeah. That essay *was* pretty incredible," Adam agreed.

"Not as incredible as the essay Tucker and I cowrote about Mr. René Descartes," Chen bragged.

"Oh, yeah? No one buys that *cogito, ergo sum* crap anymore, dude. Empiricism rules!" Jason said, slamming the table with his fist.

He, Tucker, and Chen pulled over three chairs and

crammed into the remaining spaces around the table as they continued bantering with Adam about René Descartes and someone named David Hume.

Kate took another sip of her bad, bitter latte, trying to cover up how out of it and uncomfortable she felt. She watched Adam, wondering if he had any idea how rude his friends—especially Willow—were being to her.

Her phone buzzed. She glanced at the screen, grateful for the distraction. It was a text from Chloe:

Hearts Heal e-mailed that they're looking for more volunteers. R U interested? U could drive over with me Saturdays 12–2.

Kate texted back:

Definitely! I'll talk 2 my parents when I get home and let U know.

Chloe wrote:

Where R U now?

Kate wrote:

@ Mighty Cup being miserable.

Chloe wrote:

What???? Why????

Kate wrote:

Willow is here acting like Adam's GF again. ☹

Chloe wrote:

Don't let her get 2 U. Show her who's the real GF! ☺

Kate sat up straight and pushed her shoulders back. Chloe was right. Kate needed to put a stop to Willow's weirdly territorial behavior with Adam.

Kate got up from her chair and walked over to Adam's. She took his hand, smiled, and said, "I need some air. Do you want to walk me home?"

"It would be my honor!" Adam rose to his feet and hastily stuffed his iPad and copy of Shakespeare's plays into his backpack. "Later, losers."

"Okay, Romeo," Chen teased him.

"You're just bailing because you're losing the argument," Jason added.

Willow narrowed her eyes at Kate and said nothing.

As Kate and Adam walked out of the Mighty Cup,

Adam said, "Sorry about them. They can be real jerks sometimes. But they're my best friends, and I've known them since I was, like, in diapers."

What about Willow? Is she one of your best friends, too? Or is she more than that? Kate would have liked to ask. But she didn't want to come across as a jealous, green-eyed monster.

Although if she wasn't careful, she was going to turn into just that.

CHAPTER 9

"Your father will pick you girls up later. I have my acupuncture appointment this afternoon, then an open house afterward," Mrs. Davis told Chloe as she and Kate got out of the Mercedes in front of Hearts Heal.

"Thanks, Mom!"

Chloe closed the door and watched her mother drive off. She turned to Kate and squeezed her arm. "I'm so glad you could come with me today!" she said happily. With her jam-packed schedule, she hadn't spent nearly enough time with Kate and her other friends lately.

"Yeah. I usually babysit my sibs on Saturday afternoons so my dad and Barbara can go to yoga together. But they switched to a Sunday morning class so I could do this," Kate replied.

"You're so lucky to have a big family," Chloe remarked. With Jake and Clementine off at college, it was just her and her parents around the house. Mr. Davis traveled a lot for work, and Mrs. Davis was equally busy at her real estate firm.

"I guess. I miss peace and quiet, though," Kate admitted.

"Well, if you like peace and quiet, Hearts Heal is kind of the opposite of that," Chloe warned her with a smile.

Chloe held the door open for Kate as they walked into the Hearts Heal building, then paused to rub an achy muscle in her calf. The extra-intense practices had taken a toll on her, and running their competition routine full out at the game against Medham last night hadn't helped, either. Coach Steele had insisted that the squad perform their routine as often as possible between now and Nationals, including more basketball game halftime shows as well as a special showcase for an audience of middle school students from Jefferson and Los Gatos.

Just like last Saturday, Hearts Heal was crowded and chaotic. Chloe quickly found Mrs. Hillman and introduced Kate to her.

"Thank you for so much for being here today, Kate. We can definitely use an extra pair of hands," Mrs. Hillman said gratefully. "We just got our Saturday clothing donations, and they need to be sorted. Chloe, can you take Kate through the drill?"

"No problem. Is Daniel here yet?" Chloe asked.

"He's out helping with food-pantry deliveries. He should be here soon," Mrs. Hillman replied.

Chloe took Kate to the back room and showed her what Daniel had taught her last week. As the two girls rooted through boxes and bags of clothes, Chloe thought about Daniel—and Gemma, too.

Last Monday after practice, Chloe had caught up with Gemma in the parking lot. She'd made some small talk about practice and Nationals before carefully asking her if everything was going okay for her at home. But Gemma hadn't confided in her—she'd just mumbled some excuse about having to be somewhere and taken off. Chloe had tried to talk to her a few other times during the week, but with no success.

Chloe wished she could mention all this to Kate and Emily. But if Gemma didn't want people to know about her family's money problems, Chloe knew that she shouldn't say anything to the girls.

Chloe held up a pink wool sweater and inspected it. "So . . . how are things going with your boyfriend—I mean your boy-slash-friend—Adam? Is that Willow girl still bugging you?" she asked Kate.

Kate frowned. "I get the feeling she and Adam used to

go out. I wish I could ask him, but I don't know how. I don't want him to think I'm insecure."

"Why are you?" Chloe asked her friend bluntly.

"Why am I what?"

"Insecure. You're crazy-smart, you're pretty, you're an awesome cheerleader, and you're one of the nicest people I've ever met. What do you have to be insecure about?"

Kate smiled shyly. "Thanks. I wish I were as confident as you. The thing is . . . well . . . what if Adam ends up hurting me?" Her voice broke, and her eyes stung with tears. "I mean, look at my parents. My mom cheated on my dad, and they got divorced. Then she moved three thousand miles across the country to be with her dumb boyfriend. She used to be my mom twenty-four-seven. Now she sends me an e-mail, like, once a week. Sometimes not even. What's that about?"

Chloe reached over and hugged Kate. "I know. But just because your mom disappointed you doesn't mean the rest of us are going to. And that includes Adam. I've seen the two of you together. He really, really likes you."

"Really?"

"Yeah, really. I think you can trust him."

"Oops! I'm sorry, am I interrupting a private convo?"

Chloe glanced up. Daniel stood in the doorway. He looked cute in a dusky blue polo shirt that matched the color of his eyes.

"Daniel! Hey! This is my friend Kate. She's going to start volunteering for Hearts Heal, too," Chloe explained.

Kate waved to Daniel. "Hey. Nice to meet you. Chloe's told me all about you."

"She has?" Daniel grinned at Chloe. "Did she tell you that I go through two bags of Cool Ranch Doritos a day? And that I had a major crush on Snow White when I was five?"

Chloe laughed. "Um, no?"

"Nah, just kidding. It's just one bag a day. And it was Cinderella, not Snow White," Daniel joked.

This time, Kate joined in the laughter. "That's okay. When I was in preschool, I had a crush on Peter Pan."

"Batman. Guilty," Chloe said, raising her hand.

The three of them worked together for the next hour, sorting through clothes and talking about high school. When it was almost time to go, Chloe called Daniel aside. "Can I speak to you for a sec?" she asked in a low voice.

Kate jumped to her feet. "I'm going to go find a water fountain. Plus, I want to check out the rest of this place," she said, and took off.

Daniel turned to Chloe. "What's up?"

Chloe took a deep breath. "You know Kate and I are both cheerleaders, right? And that your sister's on our squad?" she began.

"Yeah, Gemma mentioned that."

"Okay. So next week—on Saturday night, to be exact—we're having a fashion show fund-raiser," Chloe continued. "Half of the money will go toward expenses for our Nationals competition in February. And the rest of the money gets designated to the charity of our choice."

Daniel nodded. "Awesome. How can I help?"

"No, no! It's the other way around. I was wondering... well... what if we give that money to you and your family for your house?" Chloe blurted out.

Daniel's eyes widened. "Seriously?"

"Seriously. I mean, it's just an idea, and I'd have to run it by Coach Steele. But I wanted to know what you thought first."

Daniel stared down at his hands. He didn't speak for a long time.

"Wow," he said finally. "I'm kind of speechless right now. That's really generous of you. You are a cool girl, Chloe."

Chloe blushed. "Thanks," she said softly. "I know the money we raise probably won't cover much, but I figured it might at least help your parents out."

"Are you sure this money shouldn't go to another cause? There are a lot of people in Sunny Valley who could use it."

"You're right, there are. So we'll just have to keep throwing fund-raisers and raising more money," Chloe told him. "I want to talk to Coach Steele as soon as possible this week. Can you talk to your parents, too? Make sure they're okay with the idea?"

"I can talk to them tonight," Daniel told her. "Thank you, Chloe. This is, like, the nicest thing anyone's ever done for me. For my family." He added, "Does Gemma know about this?"

Chloe shook her head. "I tried to talk to her about it, but she's kind of been avoiding me. That's why I was holding off on talking to Coach Steele."

"Yeah. Gemma's had a really tough time ever since we found out about maybe losing our house," Daniel said. "I think she'll be happy to hear what you're trying to do, though—whether it works out or not."

❋

That night, Chloe sat at her desk trying to get a jump on her reading assignment for English: *A Farewell to Arms*, by Ernest Hemingway. She was a really good student, and English was one of her best subjects. But she was having trouble making sense of the complicated narrative. She made a mental note to ask Kate some questions about it at practice tomorrow; knowing her friend, she'd probably read it in middle school. Coach had confirmed at the game last night that she was definitely keeping the extra Sunday sessions between now and Nationals.

Chloe munched on an apple and glanced around her

room. It was twice the size of the main room at Hearts Heal and had its own private bathroom with a walk-in shower. The decor was blue and gold, Northside's colors. A plush indigo quilt covered her bed. Her teddy bear, Pom—who wore a blue-and-white cheerleader's uniform and clutched tiny poms—sat on a bookshelf next to her All-Star medals and framed school portraits. Across the room, French doors opened up to a balcony that overlooked the backyard, a koi pond, and an infinity pool.

There was no question about it—Chloe was lucky to have all this. The thought had never really occurred to her before she started volunteering at Hearts Heal, and before she met Daniel. She'd always known that her family was well off, but she was starting to realize that she shouldn't take her home for granted.

A *ding* sounded on her computer. There was an instant message from Emily:

> **ShinyEmily:** lined up 5 more boutiques for the fashion show!!!!! ☺
> **TimberChloeD:** emmmmm, awesome. way 2 go ☺
> **ShinyEmily:** getting down to the wire. it's next sat.!!!!! eeeeeek!!!!!
> **TimberChloeD:** what can I do?

> **ShinyEmily:** just be at my house tomorrow at 5 ok? to help finish up posters and everything. Devin and Kate will be here.
> **TimberChloeD:** I'll be there!!!!! ☺

Her computer dinged again. Another chat window opened up. For a second, Chloe didn't recognize the name on it:

> **GemmaDilemma:** Hey Chloe?

Chloe frowned. Then she grinned when she remembered that GemmaDilemma was Gemma Moore. Gemma almost never IM'd her.

> **TimberChloeD:** hi Gemma, what's up?
> **GemmaDilemma:** My brother told me that u guys talked 2day at HH. He told me about ur idea.
> **TimberChloeD:** yes!!!! what do you think? ☺

For a long moment, there was no reply from Gemma. Then:

GemmaDilemma: I think u should stay out of my family's business. WE DONT NEED UR HELP. And don't u dare tell ANYONE about our house or I will never speak 2 u again!!!!!

CHAPTER 10

Emily cleared a swath on her messy bed and watched as flyers, poster mock-ups, and other random stuff went falling to the floor. Flopping down on her frayed but familiar patchwork bedspread, she closed her eyes and stifled a scream of total exhaustion. She had never been more tired in her life. And her Sunday wasn't over yet—not even close!

She'd gotten up at seven AM to go to early services at church with her family. Then she'd helped out with the weekly grocery shopping. Afterward, her father had driven her downtown so she could visit the last five boutiques on her list to solicit donations for next Saturday's fashion show fund-raiser.

At two o'clock she'd had cheer practice. More like cheer boot camp, really. Coach Steele had lost her temper at the squad not once, not twice, but three times. At one point, a few of the girls had actually burst into tears and stormed off to the locker rooms. With less than three weeks to go until Nationals and their routine still far from perfect, everyone seemed to be at a breaking point.

And now...Devin, Chloe, and Kate were coming over at five so they could finish up the flyers and posters for the fashion show and also advertise the event on a bunch of social media sites.

On top of which...Travis had been texting her all day, trying to persuade her to come to a Hashtag songwriting sesh after dinner. Emily still hadn't made up her mind about whether to join the group for real. She realized that she couldn't keep Travis and the other guys waiting much longer, and she was seriously feeling the pressure.

"Emily?"

Devin popped her head through the door. "Your dad let me in. I'm a little early."

"Great. Come on in," Emily called out wearily.

Devin frowned at the sight of Emily sprawled on her bed and at the mess on her floor. "Hey, are you okay? You aren't sick again, are you? I mean, 'sick'?" She made quote marks in the air with her fingers.

"Ha-ha. No, I'm not sick. I'm just exhausted," Emily complained.

"I'm sorry. How's everything going? Did you get the rest of your outfit donations?"

Emily sighed, sat up, and propped herself against a bunch of pillows. *Time to get back to work.* She reached for her REALLY IMPORTANT STUFF notebook, which was buried under a bunch of art supplies, and flipped through the pages. When she got to the OUTFIT DONATIONS page, she quickly double-checked the total.

"Yup. Thirty outfits total," she said after a moment. "The woman at Teen Dream said she has to confirm with her boss, but she was ninety-nine percent sure they could give us this cute black dress."

Devin sank down on the bed next to her. "Awesome!"

"I know! If we can get people to bid, like, twenty-five to fifty dollars each for the outfits, that's seven hundred and fifty to fifteen hundred dollars—plus whatever we make on ticket sales," Emily calculated.

"My mom talked to her friend at the hospital. You know, the one whose husband owns the company that rents entertainment equipment? She said Mr. Viscardi would donate a catwalk stage and lights for the event," Devin told her.

Emily's eyes lit up. "Great! Major score! Please give your mom a big hug of gratitude for me."

"Will do. What about the sound system, though? We don't have one yet, right?"

"The Hashtag guys said they'd set it up and run it for us during the event."

"Wow, that's huge. Did you have to, like, promise to join the band in return?"

"No. Although..."

"What?"

"Travis has been really patient about that. We—I mean, Hashtag—is supposed to record those new songs on February sixteenth." Emily hesitated. "I honestly don't know what to do. I haven't told my parents. I haven't told Chloe or Kate. I haven't told anyone but you."

"Really?"

"Really. I'm terrified that everyone will try to talk me out of it."

"That makes it sound like you're leaning toward it."

"*Welllll*...I kind of am. I mean, what person in her right mind turns down a chance like this?"

Devin shrugged. "Don't say yes because you think you're *supposed* to. Say yes because it's what you really, really want."

"That's the problem. I don't *know* what I really, really want."

"What are you guys talking about?"

Emily glanced up quickly. Chloe was standing in the

doorway, staring at her with a curious expression. Kate was right behind her.

"Oh...hey! Hi! We were just talking about the, uh, fashion show. I'm not sure what outfit I would want," Emily improvised.

Chloe and Kate walked into the room and sat down on the bed next to Emily and Devin.

"Is it just me, or does it feel like we've all been keeping secrets from each other lately?" Chloe said slowly.

Emily and Devin exchanged a glance. "Um...okay, guilty," Emily confessed after a moment.

Devin raised her hand. "Me too," she admitted.

"Me three," Chloe added with a smile.

"Me four, sort of," Kate piped up. "I mean, I don't have a secret, exactly. But there's this girl, Willow, who's been flirting with Adam. She's a junior, too, and they're like old childhood friends or something. It really bothers me, but I didn't want you guys to think I was crazy-jealous."

"What? We can all be crazy-jealous sometimes. That's perfectly normal," Emily told her. "As for this Willow chick? Point her out to me tomorrow at school. I'll have a little talk with her and make sure she never comes near your man again."

Kate giggled. Emily, Chloe, and Devin joined in. It was good to be able to talk and laugh together, especially after everything they'd all been going through lately.

"Okay, so I'll go next," Devin volunteered. "There's this guy named Mateo—do you know him? He's on the JV basketball team. We've been working together on a project for our history class. The thing is, I think he kind of likes me. And I think I kind of like him."

"Does Josh know?" Kate asked.

Devin shook her head vigorously. "No! And it's not like I've done anything with Mateo. I'm not that girl. I don't want to *be* that girl. Besides, I really like Josh. He and I have a history."

"How are things going between you and Josh?" Emily asked.

Devin frowned. "I don't know. We still Skype a few times a week. But it's like my heart's not really in it. And neither is his." She added, "Things would be different if we lived in the same city and went to the same school, like we used to. Long-distance is so hard!"

Kate reached over and gave Devin a hug. "Don't feel bad about liking Mateo. You should be honest with Josh, though. Otherwise, he might wonder—just like I wonder about Adam and Willow."

"That's *not* the same, Kate. There is *zero* going on between Adam and Willow. She's just a big, attention-hungry flirt," Chloe pointed out.

"Maybe. Maybe not." Kate shrugged.

"IMHO? Kate, you should ask Adam if he and Willow

are just friends or what," Emily declared firmly. "Devin, you should tell Josh you like Mateo. Everyone should be honest."

Devin raised her eyebrows at Emily. "Does that include you?"

Chloe and Kate swiveled around to face Emily, too. "Come on, spill," Chloe encouraged her friend. "Kate and I know you've been keeping something from us."

Emily sighed. She picked up her stuffed Timberwolves mascot—she'd actually inherited it from Chris, who'd inherited it from Eddie—and hugged it to her chest. It smelled familiar and comforting.

Emily took a deep breath. Then she told her friends about everything that had happened over the past few weeks—including Travis's big news, the meeting with Jacinta Cruz at Rampage Records, and lying about having the flu to skip practice.

"I'm really, really, *really* sorry I lied to you guys," she finished. "I didn't know what to do. I was worried that you wouldn't understand because…well, because…you're more into cheering than anyone I've ever met, Chloe. And Kate, you're pretty fanatical about it, too. I was worried that you guys would think I was crazy for even *thinking* about quitting to try to become a rock star or whatever."

Chloe squeezed Emily's hand. "Hey, give Kate and me some credit. We both know there's life beyond cheerleading.

And you're an awesomely talented singer. You *deserve* to be a rock star."

"Awww, thanks!" Emily hugged Chloe. It was such a relief to be able to tell her friends the truth, finally.

"So what's *your* secret?" Kate asked Chloe. "You're the only one who hasn't spilled yet.

Chloe looked away. She appeared really upset. Emily hadn't seen her friend this shaken up in a long time.

"It's not my secret to tell," Chloe said after a moment. "One of the families at Northside is about to lose their home. I thought we could help them out by giving them money from the charity fashion show."

"That is a *great* idea!" Devin said enthusiastically.

"Which family is it?" Kate asked curiously.

"I can't say. Not just yet," Chloe replied.

Emily studied Chloe. "It's someone on the squad, isn't it?" she asked quietly.

Chloe didn't answer.

CHAPTER 11

"Mom! I'm home!"

Devin walked through the front door, shrugged off her NHS hoodie, and set her backpack down on the floor. She was mentally numb from the last two hours of poster-making. (STYLE WITH A CAUSE! BE GENEROUS AND BEST DRESSED!) Crafting wasn't really her thing. It was an effort for her—just like cheerleading used to be, and just like making new friends used to be.

Still, she'd had fun hanging out with the girls and talking about important girl stuff. She wondered, idly, if the family Chloe mentioned might be Gemma Moore's. She'd noticed Gemma and Chloe engaged in a few tense-looking conversations lately. In any case, Devin totally understood about money problems; she sometimes overheard her mom on the phone with their landlord, explaining why the rent was going to be late again.

It had been really nice for Devin tonight, sharing her own secrets about her growing distance from Josh as well as her tiny crush (*there, she'd said it—crush!*) on Mateo. Not that she was any closer to figuring out what to do. Part of her was tempted to break things off with Josh and be free to hang out with other boys. But another part of her wanted to try to work things out. Josh was a great guy. And when it came to relationships, she didn't want to quit, like her parents had.

Emerald bounded up and rubbed against Devin's ankles, purring. She reached down to pet the fluffy orange cat. "Hi, girl. Where's Mom?"

Emerald meowed loudly.

Then Devin remembered: her mom had gone into work this morning to cover for another nurse who was on vacation. She would be coming home any minute now, wanting dinner—and probably exhausted, since she'd pulled a double shift yesterday and hadn't returned until well past midnight.

Devin wandered into the kitchen. The sink was full of dirty dishes, and Emerald had knocked her food bowl over again. Devin cleaned it up, then loaded the dirty dishes into the dishwasher. She put a pot of water on the stove and searched through the cupboards for something to boil. There was a box of penne, and a jar of pesto, which she could toss with the cooked pasta.

Devin heard the front door open and close, and a jangling of keys. A minute later, Linda Isle walked into the kitchen.

"Hey, honey." Devin's mother peeled off her Elmo scrubs, which she wore over a denim dress, and tossed them in the general direction of the washer. She worked in the pediatric intensive care unit—or PICU, as it was called—and her scrubs always had a kid-friendly theme. "Looks like you've started dinner—thanks."

"Penne with pesto. And I think there's some spinach in the fridge that's not too gross. I can make a salad," Devin replied.

"How can I say no to not-too-gross spinach?" her mom said with a chuckle. She opened the refrigerator and pulled out a half-empty bottle of white wine. "Long day," she said, pouring herself a glass and taking a sip. "We almost lost a patient, but I think he's going to pull through. Brave little guy, he's only six years old. He's been fighting leukemia since he was three."

"That's awful! I'm glad he's doing better," Devin said.

Mrs. Isle sat down at the kitchen table. "How was your day? Cheer practice, right? And then you went over to your friend Emma's house?"

"Emily. We worked on the fashion show fund-raiser. Are you coming to that?"

"I wouldn't miss it! I switched shifts with my coworker Fran, so I'm all set."

"We made, like, a zillion posters to hang on the walls at school. Oh, and I have some flyers for you to pass out at the hospital." Devin opened the box of penne and dumped it into the boiling water.

"So are you going to be one of the runway models?" her mom asked.

"Maybe. You know me. I'm not exactly into clothes. But Emily thought I'd be a good model for this one particular dress because of my hair color. It's, like, this green velvety thing with ruffles at the top." Devin gestured vaguely around her neck area.

"Oooh, green velvet! Yes! You'll look stunning in that!"

Devin grinned. "I guess. Anyway, a bunch of us are modeling. Emily also had this crazy new idea. She thinks we should try to get a celebrity to be one of our models, to help increase ticket sales."

"A celebrity model? Yes, that *would* be nice—but how does she plan to pull that off? Is she friends with any celebrities?"

"No. But you don't know Emily. She's totally relentless. She'll pick up the phone and make five hundred calls if she has to, until she finds a celebrity who'll say yes."

Mrs. Isle smiled. "I'm really looking forward to this fashion show. I only wish I could come to Nationals as well. I'd give anything to see you out there—and I know Sage would, too," she said with a sigh.

Devin's older sister, Sage, was a legend in the cheerleading world. She'd taken her squad to Nationals when she was a senior at Spring Park High. She'd been featured in *American Cheerleader* magazine. And now she was a star on the UCLA cheer team.

Mrs. Isle wasn't just supportive of Devin being on the NHS JV cheer squad. She'd practically coerced Devin into it, scheming with her old friend Meg Steele to have "Sage's little sister" join the JV without an official try-out. Devin used to do gymnastics back in Spring Park, and Coach Steele had been eager to get someone with her experience on the team. Fortunately, it had worked out for everyone. After a rough start, Devin had grown to enjoy being a cheerleader. And she liked to think that she was a strong asset to the others, especially in her role as cocaptain.

Just then, Devin's phone buzzed in her pocket. She pulled it out and glanced at the screen.

She blinked in surprise. It was a text from Josh:

Do u have a min to Skype? It's important.

Devin typed back:

Sure, give me a sec. I'll Skype u, okay?

"It's Josh," Devin announced to her mother. "He says it's important. Would it be okay if I, um—" She glanced in the direction of her room.

"Sure, honey. Skype away. I can finish getting dinner on the table," Mrs. Isle offered. "Pesto sauce, right? And a spinach salad?"

"Yup. There's dressing in the fridge. Thanks, Mom!"

As Devin hurried to her room, she wondered what was up with Josh. They already had a Skype date set for tomorrow night. What could be so important that it couldn't wait until then?

She got to her desk and booted up her outdated laptop. A few minutes later, Josh's image came to life on the screen. He sat on the edge of his bed strumming his guitar. He wore white board shorts, a tie-dyed T-shirt, and an orange-and-black San Francisco Giants cap. A hot-pink feather boa was draped around his neck.

The boa made no sense. Neither did the baseball cap, since Josh hated organized sports. Neither did his room—which, from what Devin could see, was way cleaner than usual. His bed was made, and the floor was immaculate. *Weird.*

Devin smiled and waved. "Hey, Josh."

"Hey there, Devin Isle! I really missed your smile!" Josh sang.

Devin laughed. "You singing the Sunday night blues?"

"I've got the Sunday night blues...and I can't think of a word that rhymes with bluuues," Josh sang. He stopped strumming and set his guitar down on the bed. "Lame. So how's *your* Sunday going?"

"Oh, you know. Practice was insane. It's getting so close to Nationals, and everyone's, like, totally on edge. Afterward, some of us went over to Emily's to help prep for the fashion show." Devin leaned forward. "So, um... what's up? You said it was important. And what's with the feather boa?"

"What? Oh, yeah. I borrowed it from Josie," Josh replied, referring to his three-year-old sister. "I have to bring in a bunch of props for English tomorrow. Mr. Ferguson's making us break up into groups and act out scenes from this play called *Blithe Spirit.* I'm the medium."

"The medium what?"

"You know...a medium. As in, psychic? Clairvoyant? Person who can look into the crystal ball and tell the future?"

"Oh, *that* kind of medium."

"Yeah." Josh unraveled the boa from his neck and let it flutter to the floor. "So..." He seemed to be struggling for words; Devin knew he was usually much more comfortable singing than speaking. "I'm not sure where to start," he said finally.

"Just spit it out," Devin told him.

"Okay. Here goes. I haven't been the most awesome boyfriend to you lately. And it's my fault," Josh began.

"What do you mean?" Devin said, surprised.

"You've probably noticed that I've been kind of distracted, right? The thing is...I haven't been completely honest with you."

Devin's green eyes widened. Was Josh giving her the opening she needed to be able to come clean with him, too? "Really? Because I haven't been completely honest with you, either," she said nervously.

"Okay, I want to hear your thing. But first, let me tell you my thing." Josh paused and glanced away at some point beyond his computer screen. "We've been going through some stuff."

"Yeah, I agree."

"Huh? I'm talking about my family," Josh said, confused.

Devin startled. "Wait, what?"

"Josie was diagnosed with something called Asperger's syndrome a few months ago," Josh went on. "My parents were worried because she has a hard time talking and socializing with people. They've been dealing with a ton of doctors and therapists. It's been kind of crazy around our house, and I've had a hard time focusing on anything else, including us. You and me. Our relationship."

"Omigosh!" Devin had expected Josh to break up with her. Or tell her that he'd met someone else. Anything but this news about his sweet little sister. "What can I do? I can talk to my mom. She knows a lot about children because of her work," Devin offered.

"That's really nice of you, thanks. I think my parents have it covered, though. Just keep being my Devver, okay? And if I ever space out on an anniversary or forget to send you a Valentine's Day card or whatever, just try to understand. It'll get better, I promise."

Devin felt all the air go out of her chest. She was an awful, terrible girlfriend. All these months, Josh had been worrying about his sister. And here she was, moping because things didn't "feel romantic" between them anymore.

And flirting with other guys.

Well, *one* other guy, anyway.

"So what did you want to tell *me* about?" Josh asked her.

Devin plastered on a big smile. "What? Oh, nothing. Nothing at all! Just...I know I've been distracted, too. With Nationals coming up and everything. I'm sorry if I haven't been the best girlfriend to you, either."

"Get out of here, Devver. You're the best girlfriend in the universe. In fact, I've been working on a new song about you. Here's a little preview...."

Josh picked up his guitar and began singing again. He sang about Devin's long, crazy red hair; the way she ate pizza slices backward (crust first); and the time they slow-danced outside in the rain. Listening, Devin felt like a total and complete jerk. What had she been thinking?

Obviously, she hadn't been. *Thinking, that is.*

Emerald jumped in Devin's lap and flopped onto her back. Devin stroked the cat's soft belly, just the way she liked it. Then Devin made a promise to herself. From now on, she was going to be there for Josh. Totally, 100 percent, with all her heart and soul *there*. She would do whatever it took to get Mateo out of her system.

CHAPTER 12

"Thanks for the ride, Mr. Davis! See you tomorrow, Chloe!"

Kate waved good-bye as she walked through the front yard to her house. Mr. Davis had been nice enough to drive her home from Emily's. Kate breathed in the cool night air, which was heavy with the fragrance of gardenias and other flowers. Her stepmother was a big gardener.

When she opened the front door, she expected to hear the usual dinner-hour chaos. Her stepbrothers, Garrett and Jack (six and four, respectively), and her sister, Sasha, who was two, were always a handful, but they were especially wound up and prone to tantrums at this time of day.

But there was no crying or screaming in the house. No video games or cartoons blaring on the TV.

Kate proceeded into the family room. She stopped and stared in shock.

Adam sat cross-legged on the carpet, reading a book to her three very attentive siblings. Garrett and Jack sat on either side of him, with Sasha scrunched up on his lap, cradling the new American Girl doll she'd gotten for Christmas. Their Australian shepherd, Scout, lay in front of the fireplace. He thumped his tail lazily when Kate came into the room.

Adam glanced up from the book and waved to Kate. "Hi! I dropped by to see if you wanted to go out for pizza, and your parents invited me to dinner," he announced.

"Dad and Barbara invited you to dinner?" Kate said, dumbfounded. Her stepmom was "Barbara" sometimes and "Mom" at others. Kate was still trying to figure it out. In any case, she hadn't noticed Adam's beat-up red Volvo parked out front.

"Aaaadam! Finish the stooory!" Jack demanded.

"Story, story, story!" Sasha cried out, bouncing up and down on his lap.

"*Ow!* So the clock started to strike midnight. *Bong–bong–bong!* Cinderella had been having so much fun doing the Harlem Shake with Prince Charming that she'd forgotten all about her promise to her fairy godmother."

Kate giggled. "Adam, are you changing the plot?"

Adam put his finger on his lips. "*Shhh.* Anyway, so Cinderella tore out of there," he continued, lowering his voice as his enraptured audience leaned in. "But one of her glass slippers went flying off. She didn't have time to pick it up, though, because she was worried that her Humvee stretch limousine would turn back into a pumpkin...."

Kate grinned happily. Adam seemed to be doing just fine. She set her backpack down on the floor and went into the kitchen, breathing in the aroma of coconut and basmati rice. *Yum.*

"Hey, Katie-bug." Her father, Andrew MacDonald, pecked her on the cheek. "We asked your friend Adam to stay for dinner. Hope that's okay."

"Well, of course it's okay. I'm making my famous Thai chicken curry!" Kate's stepmom piped in. She swept her bangs off her forehead as she continued stirring the curry on the stove. "How was practice today, sweetie? I picked up a couple more bags of Epsom salts at the pharmacy in case you need a nice hot bath later."

"That's awesome, thanks!" Kate said gratefully. Coach Steele always advised the girls to take nightly baths to relieve their sore muscles. "Can I help with anything?"

"You can set the table. Garrett, Jack, and Sasha already ate. But they can sit with us and have some fruit salad. They're all madly in love with Adam." Barbara glanced up and smiled warmly. "He seems very nice."

Kate blushed. "Yeah. He is."

"So...he's two years older than you, right? How long have you known each other? Would you call him a good friend, or is he more like a—" Mr. MacDonald began.

"*Dad!*" Kate cried out.

"*Andy!*" Barbara said at the same time.

Mr. MacDonald held up his hands and laughed. "Okay, okay. I won't argue with the women of this house. I was just curious."

"Can we *pleeease* change the subject?" Kate begged.

"Sure, honey. Hey, did I tell you about the new park we're thinking of building down by the waterfront? We got a big grant...."

As her father talked about his job as a city planner, Kate began pulling forks, knives, and chopsticks out of the drawer. One, two, three grown-up place settings. Four, including Adam.

Even though she didn't want to talk about it with her dad, Kate was also wondering if she and Adam were just good friends...or something more. And she still didn't know what was going on between him and Willow. But for tonight, none of that mattered. Adam was here, and her family liked him, and they were about to sit down and have dinner. Kate would talk about cheerleading practice and the fashion show and Nationals. Adam would tell funny stories about their English class. The little kids would throw grapes at one another as her dad and Barbara held hands under the table.

Maybe fairy tales do come true, Kate thought in wonder.

❋

After dinner, Kate walked Adam outside so they could say good night.

"I had a really great time tonight," Adam told her. "Your dad and stepmom are awesome. Garrett, Jack, and Sasha are awesome, too. Look, Sasha even gave me a souvenir!" He held up his arms and displayed the dozen or so farm animal stickers that Sasha had placed all over them.

Kate laughed. "That's a huge compliment. Sasha's on the sticker ratings system. One sticker means 'you're okay,' two stickers is 'you're my friend,' three stickers is 'you're my best friend,' and so on. Which means that you're *way* up there."

"Huh. So how many stickers would *you* give me, Kate?" Adam reached over and touched her face.

Kate shrugged and smiled. "Oh...I don't know. What do you think?" she joked.

"A *lot*." Adam's hand curled around to the back of her neck. He pulled her in for a kiss.

Kate's heart raced. Her stomach felt fluttery. Time seemed to stop as Adam's lips brushed ever so softly against hers.

Then, all of a sudden, the image of Willow flashed darkly through Kate's head. Willow, with her long auburn hair and cool glasses and tight T-shirts. Willow, who acted like Adam belonged to her.

Jealousy washed over Kate, and she turned abruptly and stared at the ground.

"Hey. What is it?" Adam asked her.

"Nothing," Kate mumbled.

"No, it's not nothing. *Tell* me."

Kate bit her lip. "It's Willow," she admitted.

Adam frowned. "Willow? What about her?"

"Are the two of you...I mean, did you ever...I mean..." Kate stopped, flustered.

"Are you asking if Willow and I ever went out?"

Kate nodded mutely.

"The answer is *nein. Nyet. Non.* That's no in German, Russian, and French," Adam replied. "I can keep going in other languages, if you want."

Kate glanced up. Hope flickered in her chest.

"Seriously, though. Willow's lived next door to me since forever," Adam explained. "Her parents and my parents are good friends—you know, backyard barbecues, block parties, et cetera, et cetera. I know she's not the easiest person in the world to deal with. I think it's a defense-mechanism thing. But under all those layers of weirdness, she's okay. She can even be nice sometimes."

Kate wrinkled her nose. "I can't picture Willow being nice."

"Give her time. Besides, she's not interested in me. I heard she's got a big fat crush on Sebastian Smith, the guy on the tennis team," Adam added.

"Really?" Kate mulled this over.

"Really. Anyway, do you feel better now?" Adam asked her.

"A little." Kate added, "She definitely doesn't like me, though. None of your friends do. They think I'm a dumb cheerleader or whatever."

"I'm sorry they're being such jerks," Adam apologized. "I'll talk to them."

"No, don't! I just don't want anyone to think I'm the difficult girlfriend who always complains," Kate said quickly.

"Girlfriend?" Adam repeated, raising his eyebrows.

Kate blushed furiously. "I meant to say 'friend.'"

"Actually, I kinda liked 'girlfriend' better," Adam said.

Kate stared at him. He stared back.

"Okay, I really want to kiss you now," Adam whispered, leaning in.

This time, she let him.

CHAPTER 13

Chloe took a deep breath. Every cell of her being was focused on the tumbling pass she was about to perform. *Ready, set, go!* She sprinted across the mat, paused to get into position, then executed a round-off, handspring, tuck. *Yes!*

"Way to nail it, Davis," Coach Steele said, clapping from the sidelines. "You might want to try to get your feet together faster in your round-off for some more speed. Otherwise, that was terrific."

"Thanks, Coach!" Chloe trotted back to the corner of the gym to join the other cheerleaders.

"You looked so good!" Kalyn Min told her.

"Agreed. With your mad tumbling skills, you're practically ready for the Olympics!" Jenn Hoffheimer added.

Chloe grinned, pumped from all the praise. "Thanks, guys! Your passes were awesome, too!" she said.

Chloe wiped her brow with the back of her T-shirt and stretched her arms. The extra practices these past few weeks had been tough on everyone's schedules, but she could tell that they were paying off. Everyone's tumbling had improved since the holidays, and so had the rest of the Nationals routine.

Which was a good thing, since the competition was just over two weeks away. And once they were in Orlando, they wouldn't have a gym for practicing. At Nationals, teams usually practiced on the grassy areas outside their hotels or the ESPN competition venue. There were only so many gyms in the city that had availability for all the visiting teams, and those spaces tended to get booked months in advance.

Devin went next, performing the same pass as Chloe but substituting a layout for the back tuck. Chloe knew that Devin had been working on that extremely difficult maneuver all season. Devin stuck the tricky landing cleanly, without a single extraneous movement, and finished with her arms in a triumphant V and a wide grin on her face. Then she lowered her arms quickly, probably remembering that the V was a gymnast thing, not a cheer-leader thing.

Everyone in the gym broke out in whistles and claps, including a few of the JV basketball players who were practicing on the other side of the room. Chloe noticed Mateo Torres among them, whistling and clapping a little louder than the others. *He's definitely cute*, she thought. *No wonder Devin's got a crush on him.*

Not that Devin seemed like the type of girl who fell for guys just because of their looks. Still, she wondered what Devin planned to do about her Josh-Mateo dilemma. Last night at Emily's, she'd been going on and on about how smart and nice Mateo was. But this morning during homeroom, Devin had said the same about Josh. What was going on?

Gemma went next. After she'd completed her pass, she got in line behind Devin.

Chloe gave Gemma a thumbs-up sign. "That was awesome," Chloe complimented her. "Your landing was really clean!"

Gemma frowned and turned away.

"What's wrong with Gemma?" Devin whispered to Chloe.

"I don't know," Chloe whispered back. But of course, she *did* know.

She had to talk to Coach Steele ASAP about Gemma and her family. After all, the fashion show was this Saturday.

◆

"What did you want to discuss, Davis?" Coach Steele asked.

Practice was over. As Chloe sat across from the coach's desk, she tried to remember the speech she'd rehearsed over and over in her mind—about meeting Daniel at Hearts Heal and learning about the Moore family's dilemma. It wasn't easy pitching a particular charity to Coach Steele, since there were so many worthy charities in Sunny Valley. Chloe had to convince Coach Steele that the squad should devote half their fashion show earnings to help the Moores save their home—even though Gemma didn't *want* their help.

Chloe glanced around the coach's cramped office. Her desk was piled high with papers, files, and rule books. Trophies dating back two decades lined the bookshelves. Motivational posters covered the walls with sayings like MAKE IT YOUR GOAL TO OUTDO YOURSELF, NOT OTHERS and BE A LEADER THROUGH YOUR ACTIONS and DREAM BIG!

"Well?" Coach Steele prompted her. "You and Devin aren't having problems again, are you? I thought the two of you had worked things out last semester."

"No, no, it's not that at all!" Chloe took a deep breath. "It's about the fashion show. I have an idea for the charity."

"That's fantastic! What's your idea?"

"I've been doing volunteer work at Hearts Heal on Saturday afternoons," Chloe began. "Gemma Moore's brother volunteers there, too. His name is Daniel, and he's a sophomore at Sunny Valley Performing Arts. Anyway, he happened to tell me that their dad got laid off from his job a while back. Money's tight and they may have to sell their house."

Coach Steele raised her eyebrows. "*Really?* That's awful! I had no idea."

"So I was thinking... what if we give them half the proceeds from the fashion show?" Chloe went on.

Coach Steele nodded slowly, as though she were mulling it over. Chloe chewed on her thumbnail as she waited for the coach's answer.

"I think it's a fine idea, as long as the Moores are interested," the coach said finally. "I'll call them as soon as we're done here and run it by them. I know that you want to help out a teammate, which is great. But we also have to respect their privacy."

Chloe sat up straight. "Well, that's the thing—" She hesitated.

"What is it?"

"I mentioned the idea to Daniel when I saw him at

Hearts Heal on Saturday. He was very excited and grateful. I guess he mentioned it to Gemma, too. Gemma's not excited *or* grateful at all. In fact, she sent me an instant message that night and told me to stay out of her family's business. She seems pretty mad at me," Chloe confessed.

Coach Steele smiled sympathetically. "You know, it's not easy having the world know that your family is experiencing problems. Especially when those problems have to do with money. Gemma is probably embarrassed about her family's situation," she guessed.

"That makes sense," Chloe agreed.

"Let me talk to Mr. and Mrs. Moore. If they say yes, I think it would be a good idea to keep their names anonymous at the fashion show, to respect their privacy." Coach Steele folded her hands on the desk and leaned forward with a smile. The coach hadn't smiled much lately, so it felt special somehow. "I must say, Chloe—I have to commend you for coming up with the idea to help the Moores. And also for volunteering at Hearts Heal on your own time. You're acting like a true leader."

Chloe beamed. It was the second time today the coach had complimented her. And this compliment, which had nothing to do with her athletic skill, felt a hundred times more wonderful and amazing.

CHAPTER 14

"Where are the bidding paddles? Has anyone seen the bidding paddles? And omigosh, what are all those empty hangers doing over there?" Emily shouted. "I need everyone to get things in order, like, immediately. The fashion show is starting in thirty-five, no, thirty-four minutes!"

Chloe strolled over to Emily and put a hand on her shoulder. "Stressed much?" she asked sympathetically.

Emily rubbed her temples with her fingers. "A bit. It's just that so much is riding on this fund-raiser. Our early ticket sales were way short. Which means we need a *lot* more people to show up last-minute."

Chloe looked thoughtful, then pulled her phone out of

her pocket. "Let me send another tweet out to the NHS community. That might get more people here. I'll ask my mom to do the same with her real estate connections. My dad could e-mail an invite to his coworkers at his law firm."

"Yes! Good idea!"

"Where do I put these cupcakes?" cheerleader Wren Pexa asked, balancing a massive tray on her arms. "My mom and I baked, like, four dozen of them!"

"Thanks, Wren! The concession table's over there," Emily replied, pointing.

"How does my dress look?" Lexi came running up to Emily and twirled around. Lexi was petite and looked particularly adorable in the white lace sundress. "It seems like it's too big around the waist. What do you think?"

Emily gave Lexi's dress a careful once-over. "You just need a pin to take in the side seams a little. Phoebe's got some. *Phoeeebeee!*"

Kate walked by just then, carrying a large metal cash box and several rolls of tickets. "Phoebe's one of your models, remember? She's in the girls' locker room getting dressed," she told Emily.

"Oh, yeah. Kate, can *you* find Lexi some safety pins, then? I've gotta double-check my list and make sure everything and everyone are where they're supposed to be," Emily pleaded.

"No problem." Kate set the lockbox and tickets on a folding table and rushed off.

Emily pulled her clipboard from under her arm and scanned the list quickly. The catwalk stage, curtains, and lights from Mr. Viscardi's entertainment-equipment rental company. *Check.* Mr. Viscardi himself. *Check.* Five hundred folding chairs arranged in a U shape around the stage. *Check.* The sound system and crew. *Check.*

No, *uncheck.* Two of the Hashtag guys, Alex and Kyle, stood across the gym, running a sound check with their laptop. But Travis was missing. She pulled her cell out of her pocket and called his number. It went straight to voice mail.

"Alex! Kyle! Where's Travis?" she shouted, shoving her phone back in her pocket.

But the guys had put on their headphones and couldn't hear her. Emily stifled a yell and returned her attention to the clipboard. She could kill Travis later, if and when he bothered to show.

She continued down the list. At least the outfits were all here. Emily had recruited her brothers to drive around to the boutiques on Thursday and pick them up so that she, Chloe, Kate, and Devin could smooth out wrinkles with a steam iron.

Ten cheerleaders would act as models—Devin, Leila,

Kalyn, Jenn, Lexi, Carley, Arianna, Luisa Kessler, Maya Leone, and Phoebe Carter—splitting the thirty outfits between them, with some modeling four or five outfits and others modeling only one or two. It all depended on which dresses best suited which girls. The rest of the squad—Chloe, Kate, Marcy, Gemma, Wren, Aisha Jones, and Sarah Kim—had other tasks, including ticket sales, concessions, backstage, hair and makeup, and bid-spotting. Emily herself would be running the fashion show and trying to persuade people to bid as much money as possible for the outfits.

If only Emily had managed to get a celebrity to work the event! She'd failed on that front, though it hadn't been for lack of trying. She'd spent the last five days frantically making phone calls, leaving messages at every entertainment agency in Hollywood, pleading for just one of their famous clients to donate a few hours of time to the fashion show.

The result had been depressing. Apparently, the top agents of the top stars didn't return phone calls or e-mails from random high school girls. Emily wondered: Was this what Hollywood was really like? Not so much fancy swag bags and hanging out with record producers, but being ignored if you were a nobody? And if so, did she really want to be part of that world? She still hadn't given Travis an answer about pursuing Jacinta Cruz's offer.

"Emily!"

Travis strolled into the gym just then, a tall, gorgeous blond girl following closely behind.

Emily's jaw dropped as she stared at the pair. Was that why Travis was late—he'd been picking up his date for the fashion show? She took a deep breath and counted to ten. She wasn't sure if she was mad at Travis for being tardy... or jealous because he was with a beautiful girl... or a little of both.

"Nice of you to show up," Emily snapped as Travis walked over to her. "Can you please—"

Then Emily stopped. And stared. The girl looked incredibly familiar.

"Oh. My. Gawd," Emily gasped. "You're Serena Davenport, aren't you?"

"Yup, that's me!" Serena replied in a friendly voice. "You must be Emily Arellano. It's so nice to meet a fellow cheerleader! Travis has told me so much about you and the great work y'all are doing here tonight."

"He—he has?" Emily stammered.

"He has! So where's the dressing room? I'm ready to model some clothes!"

"You... are?"

Serena had once been a cheerleader for the University of Alabama. These days, though, she was better known as one of the hottest figures on the country-rock scene. She'd won *American Idol* three years earlier; since then she'd released two albums and scored a Grammy for her single "I Just Want to Be Your Star."

Emily glanced at Travis. He grinned and winked at her. So *that's* why he'd shown up late. Emily had a million questions for him, starting with...how did he know Serena Davenport? How had he persuaded her to come to the fashion show?

But the questions could wait. Emily took Serena's arm and said, "Thank you so much for being here. As Travis may have told you, half of the money we raise tonight will go toward the team's Nationals costs, and the other half will be donated to help a local family keep their home. Let me show you to the dressing rooms. There's a turquoise dress back there that's going to look *amazing* on you...."

Three hours later, Emily, Chloe, Kate, and Devin sat on the bleachers, counting the proceeds from the evening. Nearby, a bunch of JV basketball players broke down the catwalk stage. Other students helped to put away folding chairs.

The event had been a huge success. Thanks to Chloe's last-minute social networking efforts, including several tweets about Serena Davenport's appearance, the gym had been filled to standing room only with students, parents, and other people from the Sunny Valley community.

"I can't believe it. We made triple what we expected," Emily announced as she leafed through the last of the cash and checks.

"Having Serena Davenport here was huge," Devin spoke up.

Kate nodded. "Definitely! Leila's parents bid four hundred dollars for that purple dress Serena modeled. And Jenn's parents bid another five for the turquoise one."

Emily closed the cash box with a satisfied smile. "This means we'll be able to cover our remaining expenses for Nationals. And help the Moores, too," she declared. Chloe had told Emily, Devin, and Kate confidentially that the anonymous family in need was Gemma's.

Coach Steele walked over to the girls. Gemma was with her, along with a tall young guy and an older couple.

"Girls? Gemma's parents, Mr. and Mrs. Moore, really wanted to meet you," the coach explained. "Doug, Gillian, and Daniel—this is Emily Arellano, Devin Isle, Chloe Davis, and Kate MacDonald. These four girls were the main organizers of this fashion show tonight, especially Emily here. And Chloe gets the prize for coming up with the idea to make your family our beneficiary."

Mrs. Moore clasped them all in a fierce group hug. "I

can't thank you girls enough for what you did tonight," she said tearfully.

Daniel came up to Chloe and wrapped his arm around her shoulders. "Thank you," he told her in a low voice. "Actually, 'thank you' doesn't quite cut it. If I ever compose a violin concerto, I'm dedicating it to you."

"Hey, I'm counting on it," Chloe replied with a grin.

As Emily eavesdropped on Daniel and Chloe's private little convo, she noticed how incredibly cute he was. And nice. Chloe hadn't had a boy in her life since her disastrous non-relationship with her eighth-grade crush, Greg Marina. *Hmmm, Daniel might be a good candidate,* Emily thought, the matchmaking wheels spinning in her brain.

"My turn, Danny," Gemma told her brother, then turned to face Chloe. "I was such a jerk to you before. Will you ever forgive me?"

"Are you serious? *Yes!*" Chloe said eagerly. "I'm sorry if I put you on the spot. I know I can be kind of pushy sometimes."

"Yeah, I can totally vouch for that," Emily said, raising her hand.

"No one's asking you," Chloe joked. "Anyway, I'm just glad that you'll be staying in Sunny Valley. Our team needs you!" she told Gemma.

Gemma smiled and hugged Chloe. "Thanks! Now I'm ready to focus on Nationals."

Emily pumped her fist in the air. "Timber! Timber! Timber—"

"WOLVES!" Chloe, Kate, Devin, and Gemma finished.

All's well that ends well, Emily thought happily. It was a line Kate quoted a lot, from some famous play.

While everyone else continued talking about the fashion show and Nationals, Emily locked the cash box and handed it to the coach. Then she excused herself and headed in the direction of the locker rooms. She wanted to make sure that all the outfits had been picked up or packed up.

Opening the double doors that led to the main hallway, she spotted a familiar figure in the dimly lit corridor. He was sitting cross-legged on the floor and talking on his phone.

Travis.

He turned and saw her, too. He ended his call and tucked his cell into his pocket.

"Hi!" Emily said, rushing up to him. "I've been looking for you all night!"

Travis stood up and brushed his hands against his skinny jeans. "No, you haven't, Ems. You've been slammed since I got here, bossing around models and raising millions for charity," he teased her.

Emily grabbed his arm. "I just want to know. How on earth did you manage to get Serena Davenport here?" She glanced around. "And where did she go, anyway?"

"She had to leave for another fund-raiser in LA. And as for how I got her here, it was a piece of cake. You told me you wanted a celebrity model for the event. I called Jacinta Cruz to explain the situation, and she stepped up. Serena's one of their recording artists," Travis explained.

"Just like that?" Emily said in amazement.

"Just like that. It's nice to have friends in high places, isn't it?"

Emily blinked. This had to be a sign. The entire evening had to be a sign. Was the universe telling her to join Hashtag? For a moment, Emily closed her eyes and imagined herself as the next Serena. A former cheerleader turned rock star. It sounded pretty great.

Emily opened her eyes. Travis was staring at her intently. He reached out and caressed her cheek with the back of his hand.

On impulse, she stood on her tiptoes and planted a kiss on his lips.

Travis smiled. "What was *that* for?" he asked her.

"Yes," Emily told him.

"Yes . . . what?"

"Yes, I'm officially joining Hashtag!" Emily announced. "But don't you dare tell a soul until after Nationals! I don't want to distract my squad. And I have to talk to my parents first, to make sure they're okay with this. I'll rehearse with you guys as much as I can between now and when we leave for Orlando. And I'll be at the recording session on February sixteenth."

"Are you serious?" Travis asked.

"I'm totally serious."

Travis circled his arm around her waist and kissed her—a real kiss this time. When they stepped apart, Emily felt dizzy. Travis grinned, looking pleased.

Former cheerleader, rock star, girlfriend, Emily thought happily.

CHAPTER 15

The night air was cool as Devin stepped outside to load more boxes into the back of Emily's family's minivan. She was starving; she realized that she'd forgotten to eat dinner, although she had a vague memory of munching on baby carrots just before the event started. No wonder... Devin, Emily, Chloe, and Kate had worked all day to prepare for the fashion show, with Chloe and Kate slipping away for several hours to volunteer at Hearts Heal.

"You need help with those?" someone called out.

Devin turned. Mateo stood there, wearing a gray T-shirt and shorts, showing off his incredibly chiseled golden-brown arms and legs.

She was so taken aback to see him there that she dropped a heavy box of programs on her foot. *"Ow!"*

"Here, let me help you." Mateo rushed over, knelt down, and lifted the box from her foot. He touched her foot where the bare skin showed over the top of her sneaker and caressed it lightly. "Are you okay? Did you hurt your foot?"

His gentle touch made heat rise to her cheeks. She stepped back quickly and barked, *"I'm fine!"*

Mateo stood up, a look of confusion clouding his face. His really cute face. "Just checking. Hey, the fashion show was awesome. You all did a great job."

"You were there?" Devin asked casually.

Of course he'd been there. She'd spotted him the minute he walked into the gym and started helping out: setting up the catwalk stage, arranging the folding chairs, running around the campus searching for extension cords.

She'd also noticed him in the audience as she strutted self-consciously down the runway in her green velvet dress. (Her only preparation for her modeling gig had been to watch some fashion show clips on YouTube.) The dress had been donated by a vintage boutique called Old-School Glamour and had a low beaded neckline and sheer chiffon sleeves. Mateo had beamed and given her two thumbs up as she spun around awkwardly and disappeared behind the curtain. As she'd listened to the applause, she'd found herself wondering if Mateo liked her outfit.

"Yeah, I was there," Mateo said, smiling at her curiously. "You looked really pretty."

Devin smiled back, then felt guilty. She'd resolved to be a better, more devoted girlfriend to Josh—why did she still care what Mateo was thinking? "Um, thanks."

"You're welcome. So let me give you a hand with the rest of those."

They fell silent as they finished loading the remaining boxes into the Arellanos' van. Devin's mind raced. It had been less than a week since Josh had told her the news about his little sister, Josie. Devin had seen Mateo every day in history class. They'd also spent two study hall periods working on their mock-trial project together. For the most part, she'd managed to ignore her feelings for him. *It's just a dumb crush*, she'd told herself repeatedly. *You'll get over it. Josh needs you.*

But for some reason, tonight was different. Maybe it was the way Mateo had looked at her on the runway. Or the way he was looking at her now, as though there was something he really, really wanted to tell her.

Was it possible that he had a crush on her, too?

Mateo's voice broke into her thoughts. "Hey, Devin?"

"What?"

"Granola bar?"

"Excuse me?"

Mateo reached into his backpack and handed her a granola bar. "I thought you could use it. I heard your stomach rumbling just now."

Devin giggled with embarrassment. No wonder he'd been staring at her. "You did? I'm sorry! We were so busy today, I ended up skipping dinner," she explained.

"That's no good. What are you doing now? We could walk over to the Snack Shack," Mateo offered. "Or better yet, do you like waffles? There's a new twenty-four-hour diner around the corner, and they have the best waffles."

Oh. Devin unwrapped the granola bar and bit into it, stalling. Did he think she was hinting for him to ask her out with that stupid *I ended up skipping dinner* comment? She'd never eaten waffles late at night. It sounded fun.

But it didn't matter. She absolutely couldn't go out with him. Besides, now was her chance to establish some boundaries between the two of them, once and for all. *I'm so sorry, I meant to tell you before, but I already have a boyfriend....*

"That sounds great, but I can't," Devin said finally. "I have to...um...help Emily with some other stuff....And then her family's driving me home," she rambled on. "My mom was here, but she had to go straight to the hospital for her shift, and I promised her I'd be home by eleven, latest."

Mateo nodded. He looked a little disappointed. "Sure. Another time. See you in class on Monday."

Devin waved good-bye and stared after him as he turned and left.

I am such a jerk, she thought miserably.

※

Josh texted Devin just as she was going to bed.

Do u have time to Skype? I want to hear all about the fashion show.

Devin hesitated for a moment before she typed back:

Laptop on the fritz. Plus crazy-tired. Can we talk tomorrow?

Josh typed:

Yes. Miss u.

Devin replied:

Miss u 2.

Devin put her phone on her nightstand and clicked off the light. Emerald jumped up onto the bed and curled into a ball at her feet, purring.

Devin sighed, hating herself for having lied to Josh.

Her laptop wasn't on the fritz. She wasn't too tired to talk on the phone.

And at the moment, Josh wasn't the guy she was missing.

She was lying to *everyone* tonight—including herself.

CHAPTER 16

Kate rushed out of the locker room, feeling like a nervous wreck. The team was leaving for Orlando on Thursday, and she still had a million things to do. Plus, she was worried that she might be coming down with something; her throat felt scratchy, and her head throbbed. She probably should have stayed home, but she hadn't wanted to skip her English test or her algebra quiz. She was already missing three days of school for Nationals, and she didn't want to fall further behind.

The past week and a half since the fashion show had been a frenzy of practices, showcases, tumbling classes, one game, and two meetings with the choreographer to make last-minute tweaks to their routine. Today was their last regular practice before Nationals. Coach Steele had given the girls tomorrow off so their muscles would have a break and they could rest up for the trip.

Of course, Kate hadn't even started packing yet. Even though she was organized with her schoolwork, packing for trips was something she always left until the last minute.

And right now, she was daydreaming of curling up in bed with a good book, instead of figuring out what outfits would be right for the Orlando weather.

"Hey, Kate?"

Kate turned around. Willow, Adam's friend, stood there smiling at her. She was wearing a green peasant top and funky jeans that Kate would never dream of wearing.

Kate took a deep breath and tried to look friendly. Adam wanted to be with her, not Willow. Kate got that now. But that didn't mean that she had to be friends with Willow, did it?

"Hey, Willow. I like your top," Kate managed.

"Thanks! Are you busy? Do you have time to go for a cup of coffee?" Willow asked her.

Kate hesitated. Why did Willow want to hang out with her?

Willow seemed to sense her hesitation. "Look, I feel like you and I got off on the wrong foot. You're important to Adam, and he's my friend. I want us to get along."

"Oh! I really appreciate that, Willow. It's just that we're leaving for Nationals the day after tomorrow, and I have to go home and pack, and—" Kate began.

"Which is all the more reason you need a little break. It'll be fun—just us girls, I promise!" Willow said sweetly.

Kate ran through her mental to-do list. *Go home, set the table for dinner, help with Garrett and Jack's bedtime, walk Scout, do two hours of homework, do a load of laundry, pack, then go to bed.* Which meant that she had zero time for coffee with Willow.

Willow grabbed her wrist. "Come on. My treat. I *really* want to hear more about Nationals! Adam told me they're going to close Hollywood Studios on the last night and throw a private party for all the cheerleaders who, you know, cheer-led. I've never even *been* to Disney World. You are soooo lucky...."

I'll only stay for a minute, Kate thought as she glanced around the Mighty Cup. Emily's brother Eddie wasn't behind the counter tonight. In fact, Kate didn't recognize a single person at the café.

Willow walked over with two identical cups and set

one down in front of Kate. "It's a double-shot macchiato, my favorite," Willow explained. "My family and I drank these constantly when we went to Venice for Carnevale last year."

Kate blinked. "What's Carnevale?"

"You don't know? It's their version of Mardi Gras. Big street celebration, lots of fancy costumes and masks, everyone acting wild and crazy!"

"Oh." Kate took a sip of the macchiato. *Ugh.* It was even more bitter and unpleasant than the latte she'd had here with Adam.

"Anyway...tell me about this Nationals thing. Is this your first big competition?" Willow asked.

Kate shook her head. "No. We had to compete in Regionals down in LA last November to qualify. The whole thing was actually sort of stressful because my friend Chloe—she's one of the captains—sprained her ankle right before and had to sit out. And then our friend Emily almost didn't make it in time. But everything worked out in the end. We came in second place."

"Cool. Second place suits you." Willow tipped back her cup. "Have you always wanted to be a cheerleader?"

"Um, yeah, basically," Kate replied, still processing Willow's backhanded insult. "Chloe, Emily, and I have been best friends since we were in elementary school. Chloe's older siblings were these superstar cheerleaders at

Northside. I guess the three of us looked up to them. We wanted to *be* them."

"I never saw the appeal of cheering myself, but I can respect it," Willow remarked, pushing her glasses up her nose.

Kate frowned. She wasn't sure if that was a compliment or another weird insult. Or a little of both. Maybe it was time to change the subject. "What do you like to do, Willow?"

"Hmmm, let's see. I love movies, especially anything foreign or horror. Astronomy, philosophy, and linguistics are my favorite subjects; I took them last summer at the university. And I'm in the NHS debate club, too."

"I know. So is Adam. He really likes the teacher in charge. Mr. Foster, right?"

"Yeah, Foster's tolerable. Adam and I are thinking of switching to drama club, though. They meet on the same nights."

Kate was startled. She had no idea that Adam was interested in the drama club. "Really? He hasn't mentioned that," she said out loud.

"He probably just forgot. Auditions for the spring play are next week. *Romeo and Juliet.* He's going to try out for the part of Romeo, and I'm going to try out for Juliet. We've been rehearsing a lot after school," Willow said.

"You...have?"

"I swear, that boy is such a good actor," Willow gushed. "And he's an amazing kisser, too. But you probably already knew that, right?"

Kate froze. "I'm sorry . . . *what*?" she finally managed.

"He and I have been rehearsing act one, scene five. The part where Romeo and Juliet have their own private party after the Capulets' banquet? 'If I profane with my unworthiest hand / This holy shrine, the gentle fine is this: / My lips, two blushing pilgrims, ready stand / To smooth that rough touch with a tender kiss.' Soooo romantic!"

Kate felt her cheeks burn and a pit form in her stomach.

"Hey, Kate? Are you okay?" Willow asked, her blue eyes wide. "It doesn't bother you, does it? The thought of Adam and me kissing? Seriously, it's no big deal."

This can't be happening, Kate thought.

"Besides, you two aren't exclusive, right?" Willow pressed.

Kate shook her head numbly.

"That's what I thought! I'm so relieved, because he's coming over this weekend to hang out. You know, while you're at Nationals?"

No, no, no.

Willow smiled innocently. "Don't worry. It's just a kiss for rehearsal. It doesn't mean anything."

Kate stood up quickly, knocking over her awful cup of macchiato. Everyone in the café stared.

Willow handed her a napkin. "Oh, no, Kate! Are you okay? Did I say something to upset you?"

Kate didn't answer. She picked up her bags and ran out of the Mighty Cup, fighting back tears.

And not succeeding.

CHAPTER 17

"Oh. My. Gawd," Emily exclaimed. "I can't believe we're really here!"

Chloe leaned across her friend and craned her neck to peer out the window. A long red, white, and gold sign that spelled out ESPN WIDE WORLD OF SPORTS welcomed the Disney's Magical Express bus that had picked up the NHS JV cheerleaders, Coach Steele, and half a dozen parent chaperones (including Chloe's mom and dad) at Orlando International Airport. Palm trees swayed in the balmy breeze as the bus turned and headed toward the girls' hotel. Chloe spotted a couple of great blue herons grazing on a grassy patch by a pond. In the distance, the Florida sky was dusky and pink as the sun set on the horizon.

Chloe lifted her phone to the window and snapped a bunch of pictures in rapid succession. She planned to post photos from the trip on a Tumblr she had created for the JV team.

Coach Steele spoke briefly to the bus driver, then half stood and turned to face her cheerleaders. "Listen up, ladies! We'll be at Disney's All-Star Sports Resort in just a minute," she called out. "I'm sure I don't need to remind you to stay close together and not to wander off. You're not here to explore. You're not on vacation. We've been traveling all day, so we will be taking it easy tonight. Our agenda is as follows: we will check into the hotel, unpack our bags, eat a healthy dinner at the food court, and go to bed early. Is that understood?"

"Yes, Coach!" everyone yelled.

"Good." Coach Steele turned and sat back down. The girls resumed gabbing and taking pictures of the passing scenery.

"I'm so excited I might pee my pants," Emily said to Chloe, practically bouncing up and down in her seat.

Chloe laughed. "Please don't, since I'm sitting next to you! Although I know exactly what you mean. And we haven't even gotten to our hotel yet. Or the Field House!" she reminded her friend.

The Nationals competition would take place in several different stadiums at the ESPN Wide World of Sports Complex. Their team would be competing in the Field House, which was the biggest. Chloe had already checked out the entire complex online. The images of the Field House were really spectacular—and a little intimidating, too. The place was *huge*!

Chloe had also taken a look at the Disney's All-Star Sports Resort's website. The hotel looked super-fun. Everything there was sports-themed, from the decor to the dining. The food court where they would be eating was called the End Zone.

Leila leaned across the aisle and smiled coolly at Chloe and Emily. "My family comes to Disney World on vacation, like, every year. So this isn't that exciting for me," she announced.

"That's so interesting, Leila. Thank you for reminding us all how special you are," Emily replied sarcastically.

Leila narrowed her eyes at Emily—and Chloe, too. But Chloe wasn't fazed. Not even Leila's attitude could ruin her good mood. They were at Nationals! As far as Chloe was concerned, today was the first day of what promised to be the best, most exciting weekend of her life—no matter what the outcome.

❀

The hotel lobby swarmed with hundreds of cheerleaders, along with coaches, parents, and random fans. Chloe saw a few groups of girls outside, practicing their stunts on the grass as a crowd looked on.

I guess those girls aren't taking it easy tonight, she thought, a little nervously.

She spotted the Breckenridge team across the lobby. Their top-of-the-line teal, white, and glittery orange jackets and matching pants were unmistakable.

Breckenridge was Northside's number one rival back home. Ironically, their coach, Bryan Regan, was Coach Steele's old friend and college teammate. He had coached for Northside years ago, before leaving to work for the Bulldogs. The administration had hired Coach Steele to fill his spot and bring the Timberwolves cheerleaders back up to elite status.

Chloe saw Coach Regan rounding up his team as they checked in. She also saw their captain, Karen Gelb, taking pictures with her phone. Chloe had met Karen at cheer camp last year and not come away with a good impression. Among other things, Karen had acted totally smug about the fact that the Breckenridge girls won the Top Banana, the camp's highest honor, at the end of the summer session.

Which had made it all the more satisfying when Northside came in second place at Regionals in November, and Breckenridge came in third. But that didn't mean Chloe and her teammates could coast on that victory. No doubt Breckenridge had been training extra-hard since Regionals. Chloe had noticed how clean their routine was at their recent basketball game—they'd been *scary* good.

"Hey...Chloe, right?"

Chloe glanced up to see Karen Gelb walking toward her.

"Yup, that's me. You're Karen, right? I think we met at camp," Chloe replied, not sure what else to say.

"Uh-huh. It's nice to see you guys here." Karen lifted her phone in the air and aimed it at Chloe and several other Northside girls who were standing around. "Smile!"

Chloe smiled automatically. Why was Karen taking their picture?

"This is going on my Tumblr," Karen explained. "Hashtag loserteams. What do you think?"

Really? "I think that if that's the best you can come up with, my team has nothing to be afraid of," Chloe shot back.

Karen's eyes widened. She shrugged and tucked her phone into her pocket, as though she couldn't come up with a suitable response.

Score one for Northside, Chloe thought triumphantly.

❋

The next morning, after a light breakfast, Coach Steele led the girls to the sign-in and registration area, which was a short walk from their hotel. It consisted of three large tents and a red carpet, just like the ones celebrities had for their premieres and parties.

"We're famous!" Emily announced as she stepped onto the red carpet.

Chloe giggled. She'd never been on a red carpet before.

There were cheerleaders everywhere they looked. Many of them sported temporary tattoos of their school mascots on their cheeks. Some of their chaperones had mani-pedis that matched their school colors.

Chloe spotted Di Paige, the captain of the Madison High Spartans JV squad, coming out of one of the tents. The Spartans, who were from Akron, Ohio, were on the same floor at the hotel. In fact, the two teams had shared a row of tables at the food court last night and traded stories about their respective cheer programs.

"Hi, Chloe!" Di waved energetically. "Isn't Disney amazing? Don't you just want to live here?"

"Definitely!" Chloe was glad to see Di, who seemed really nice.

"Gotta hit the gift shop. See you later!" Di waved again and took off.

Just then, a blond girl with a clipboard came up to the Northside group. She wore a black polo shirt and khaki pants, and her name tag indicated that she was Katelyn from UCA, the Universal Cheerleaders Association. "Welcome to Nationals!" she told the NHS squad in a friendly voice.

"We're glad to be here. Where can we sign in?" Coach Steele asked.

"You can start at the tent on your right," Katelyn replied, nodding her head. "Someone will check in your team and explain all the rules about your stay here at Disney. Afterward, be sure to visit the tent on your left. That's the Family Zone, which features a bunch of free goodies from our sponsors, plus jewelry-making and other fun crafts. Finally, the tent up ahead is literally *the* most awesome gift shop for cheer gear! Enjoy!"

"Best. Vacation. Ever," Jenn remarked breathlessly to Chloe. Marcy, Kalyn, and Wren nodded in agreement as they stared wide-eyed at the scene around them.

"I know, right? But don't forget what Coach said. We need to stay focused," Chloe reminded her teammates.

Nearby, Devin raised her arms in the air. "Go, Timberwolves!" she cried out.

"GO, TIMBERWOLVES!" the other seventeen girls repeated loudly.

Inside the first tent, Coach Steele took charge of the registration process. Another black-and-khaki-clad girl—this one's name tag said ANN-MARIE—explained the rules to

Chloe and the rest of the squad. They included quiet hours from ten PM to ten AM, always traveling with a buddy, and no hanging posters on the hotel room walls.

"And, most important, there's no stunting on concrete, especially the sidewalks, parking lots, and streets," Ann-Marie finished. "During your time here, you'll see a lot of the teams stunting on the grassy areas. That's okay. We understand that practice space is not easy to come by. And, of course, you'll get a chance to warm up inside the Field House or one of the other arenas before you compete. Just remember: safety first."

Next, Coach Steele led the Northside girls across the red carpet to the Family Zone tent. Booth after booth offered free goodies like lip gloss, hair bows, and cute pins. Chattering excitedly, the girls grabbed their swag bags and began going from booth to booth to fill them up.

Chloe noticed Kate lingering by a potted palm tree, checking her phone with a worried expression. Chloe walked over to her. "Hey, Kate. What's up? Are you ready to do some 'shopping'?" she joked.

Kate glanced up. "What? I was just checking my messages."

"More texts from Adam?" Chloe asked her gently. On the plane ride, Kate had filled Chloe in on her awful conversation with Willow.

Kate nodded unhappily. "He keeps calling, too. He wants to know why I'm not answering."

"Why aren't you?"

"Maybe because I never want to see him or speak to him again?" Kate pointed out. She pulled a tissue from her pocket and blew her nose. "Sorry. I'm still not over the cold Sasha gave me. As if my life wasn't complicated enough already. I've been drinking orange juice and tea nonstop."

"Awww." Chloe gazed at her friend sympathetically. "I really think you should talk to Adam and get his side of the story first," she suggested. "What if Willow's lying? From everything you've told me before, Adam sounds like a great guy. Are you willing to break up with him forever based on some random girl's lies?"

"She's not some random girl. She's, like, one of his best friends from when they were little," Kate mumbled.

"That doesn't mean she's not lying about their relationship now. *Please* talk to Adam before you drive yourself any crazier. I hate to see you so miserable. Plus, we have a big weekend ahead of us. You need to be in a good place mentally," Chloe pointed out.

"I know, I know," Kate said with a sigh. "I can't talk to Adam right now. I just can't. But I'll check out the free stuff with you. Maybe that'll cheer me up."

As they headed for the first booth, Chloe sneaked a worried glance at Kate. Was she really okay? It wasn't always easy for Chloe to balance being a friend with being the team's cocaptain. On the one hand, she wanted to help

Kate because she cared about her. That's what friends did for each other. On the other hand, Chloe needed Kate to shake her bad mood and her boy problems so she could perform her best on Saturday.

Which was *tomorrow*.

Chloe blinked and took a deep breath as Kate picked up a tube of lip gloss and tucked it into her swag bag. Kate made a comment about the peachy color, but Chloe wasn't listening. She was already thinking ahead to tomorrow. At exactly nine AM, the JV squad would be fanning out on the Field House floor and performing their routine in front of thousands of people. And, more important, in front of the judges who would advance them to the finals—or not.

Were they ready?

CHAPTER 18

Emily was silent as she sat on the bus heading over to the Field House on Saturday morning. She was practicing a visualization technique Devin had taught her recently. She closed her eyes and mentally went through the entire Nationals routine. She imagined herself running through the first tumbling pass, then the second. She imagined herself executing a perfect liberty.

Emily's eyes fluttered open. She felt more serene now, not as nervous as she had when she'd woken up and realized that today was *the day*.

Emily's phone buzzed. She glanced at the screen. It was a text from Travis:

Yo, Ems! Good luck today. BTW we made some changes to "You're the One for Me." ❤

Emily read the message once, twice, three times...then tucked her phone back in her duffel bag without composing a reply. She couldn't face Travis at the moment.

After the fashion show, she'd told her parents about joining Hashtag, and they hadn't been happy. They'd reminded her how important high school was and how important cheering had always been to her; did she really want to put those priorities aside to pursue a professional music career? They said that there would be a family discussion once Emily returned from Nationals.

And with that, Emily had gone right back to questioning her decision to join Hashtag. She wanted her parents' support. Maybe they would come around. Maybe Emily would have a brilliant epiphany and everything would become crystal clear. In the meantime, she didn't want to disappoint her new boyfriend. Technically, she and Travis hadn't DTR'd, but things were heading in that direction. And she definitely didn't want the musical opportunity of a lifetime to slip through her fingers.

But none of that was important right now: not Travis, not Hashtag, not Jacinta Cruz, not her parents...and not the fact that once the squad returned to Sunny Valley,

Emily would have exactly five days to help organize the entire Valentine's Day dance. Her focus had to be on the competition.

The bus stopped at a circular driveway. Coach Steele got out first, followed by the rest of the squad. Everyone's blue-and-gold uniforms looked perfectly fresh and crisp, and their high ponies, white ribbons, and temporary Timber-wolf paw tattoos were pristine, too.

Dozens of other buses were parked nearby. Cheerleaders in their matching uniforms moved as one toward the competition arenas.

This is it, Emily thought.

✸

The inside of the Field House was massive, and it buzzed with energy from the crowd. As the NHS squad trailed behind Coach Steele onto the second-floor balcony that overlooked the arena, they were met by an overwhelming wall of sound. A large JV team from Kentucky performed their routine on the floor as a Rihanna mix blasted over the speakers. Huge monitors hung above the girls, flashing GOODRICH GOPHERS, LEXINGTON, KENTUCKY in tall black letters. There were TV cameras everywhere. Two rows of judges sat way in the back at long tables, their heads bent low as they took notes on the Gophers' routine.

Behind the Goodrich cheerleaders was a giant backdrop shaped like a castle, which Emily remembered from the pictures Chloe had shown her online. Thousands of fans filled the stands, waving banners and foam fingers in the air. The Gophers' hometown fans were seated in a special section on the floor. During the cheer part of the routine, they shouted back at the tops of their lungs. Other Gophers fans who were seated up in the bleachers shouted back as well. Emily knew that the judges would be scoring partly on how well the squad was able to rev up the crowd. It seemed unfair that the Gophers could bring so many fans to the competition; after all, Kentucky was way closer to Orlando than Sunny Valley, California! Chloe's parents would be in the audience, along with Leila's and Jenn's—but that would be it for the Timberwolves' fan section.

"This...is...crazy," Devin whispered, glancing around the arena.

Emily nodded. "Uh-huh."

"They're really, really good," Kate spoke up, pointing to the Goodrich squad.

"Yeah, their stunts are amazing," Chloe added with an anxious edge in her voice.

"Don't worry about them. Our routine rocks! We should stay positive," Devin reminded Chloe.

Chloe grinned. "Thanks, cocaptain! I needed that."

Coach Steele put her hands on Devin's and Chloe's shoulders. "I'm counting on *both* my cocaptains to lead our team to victory today," she said proudly.

"Yes, Coach!" Chloe and Devin replied in unison.

The NHS squad proceeded down a set of stairs and through heavy curtains to a backstage area the size of a gymnasium. In one corner, a photographer was shooting team photos against a large white backdrop. The rest of the gym was taken up by teams running their routines on side-by-side mats—each team had ten minutes to warm up.

Emily noticed several adults in matching light blue shirts carefully watching the warm-ups. "Who are they?" she asked Coach Steele, pointing.

"They're rules officials. They're making sure the squads are doing the routines correctly," the coach explained. "If not, they can force a team to change their routine last-minute or even disqualify them. They're very strict about that here."

Gulp! "Our routine is okay, though, right?" Emily said worriedly.

"Yes, of course," the coach replied tersely.

The Timberwolves watched as an official approached one of the teams and asked them to repeat their pyramid sequence. Emily wondered why; it had looked perfect.

A few minutes later, it was the Northside squad's turn to get their team picture taken. Then it was time to hit the mats for their warm-up!

The girls fanned out on one section of the floor. Chloe nodded to give the signal to start the routine. Spotters, all wearing navy shirts, assumed their positions at the backs of the mats to ensure the safety of the cheerleaders.

A minute into their practice, Emily briefly glimpsed one of the rules officials making some notes on his clipboard. As soon as the squad finished, the official hurried up to Coach Steele and spoke to her.

After the official left, Coach Steele turned to the team. "He asked our back spots to make sure they're catching the necks and shoulders of the top girls. Also, please don't step to the side on cradles. That's against the rules," she announced. "These are small but important technique reminders. Back spots, are you listening?"

"Yes!" the girls replied.

"Good. Are we all ready to compete?"

"*Yes!*" the entire squad shouted.

It was their turn to go out on the *real* floor.

Coach Steele gathered the squad in a close huddle as

they stood in a long hallway with their signs and poms, waiting for the announcer to call the team's name. Kalyn, Marcy, Arianna, and several other team members were praying quietly. Others, like Phoebe, Wren, and Carley, looked queasy. Emily reached over to squeeze Chloe's hand. Chloe squeezed back.

"This is it, ladies," Coach Steele said in a solemn voice. "You've worked very, very hard to get to this place. Remember what you've accomplished. Remember who you are. Remember your family. Your family is this team. Go, Timberwolves!"

"*GO, TIMBERWOLVES!*" the girls shouted.

Then Coach Steele left the squad as they headed down a tunnel toward the performance arena, and suddenly the whole thing felt very real. Emily heard the announcer call for Northside. Chloe and Devin led the way through the heavy black curtains that separated the backstage area from the arena. All eighteen girls spilled out in front of the giant castle, set their signs and poms down in a neat line, and scattered to their positions on the floor.

The lights were blindingly bright. Emily could barely see the audience or judges. But it didn't matter. All that mattered was that her squad execute their routine with every ounce of strength, grace, and spirit they had—and then some.

The music began. Chloe turned and nodded once with a dazzling, confident smile. The squad launched into their toe touch handsprings, losing themselves in the sheer power and magic of moving as one.

❀

Several hours later, the announcer named the JV teams who would be proceeding to finals later that day. All forty competing teams spread out on the floor in a wide semicircle, holding hands and bowing their heads.

"...and the last team to go to finals is...the Northside Timberwolves from Sunny Valley, California!" the announcer's voice boomed.

The team went crazy, jumping up and down. Emily, Chloe, Kate, and Devin fell against one another in an exhausted and ecstatic group hug. Sarah and Maya burst into tears. Coach Steele looked pleased at first, then grim.

"Listen up, ladies. Congratulations. You all deserved this," the coach told the girls. "But I'm cutting our celebration short. The final sequence needs work. Grab some Gatorade. Then let's hit the grass outside!"

Emily leaned over to Chloe. "What does she mean, the final sequence needs work?" she whispered in a low, anxious voice.

"I don't know. Maybe she just wants to fine-tune?" Chloe guessed.

Emily frowned. Her muscles hurt, and she was tired. And Kate looked as though she was ready to pass out; her cold was obviously getting worse.

Could the squad keep up their momentum and repeat their incredible performance?

CHAPTER 19

Half an hour before the NHS JV team was due back out on the floor for finals, Devin retreated into the ladies' room and locked herself in one of the stalls.

She sat down on the toilet, just thinking. And worrying. Their semifinal round had been practically flawless that morning. She knew because they had watched their routine on a video monitor backstage right after leaving the floor. The team had never nailed the stunts so well or executed such seamless tumbling passes.

But Devin wasn't so sure they'd be able to repeat that epic performance for the final round. For one thing, Kate's cold was quickly getting worse. She'd been drinking tons of orange juice and hot tea and taking echinacea as well, but she hadn't improved.

And, bottom line, Devin had a bad feeling that something would go wrong during finals. She'd tried to shake it, but she wasn't succeeding. Part of it had to do with the fact that she'd forgotten to pack her lucky socks. She knew it was stupid to dwell on a superstition like that. But Sage *always* wore her lucky socks during meets and competitions. Devin had started the same tradition last fall, with her first game cheering for the Timberwolves.

Her phone buzzed. She pulled it out of her duffel bag and realized quickly that she had two texts: one from Josh and one from Mateo. They'd obviously seen the Nationals news on Twitter. Both wished her good luck, though Josh added *O*s and *X*s.

So why did Mateo's message make her heart beat faster?

Devin tucked her phone away. She couldn't be thinking about her crazy, complicated love life now, when she had much bigger issues.

"Devin? Are you in here?"

Devin's head jerked up as she recognized Emily's voice just outside the stall.

"Yes!" Devin unlocked the door and pushed it open with her shoe.

Emily stood there and stared at Devin curiously. "You're obviously not peeing. So what's up?"

"I'm thinking," Devin replied.

"About...?"

"About how to follow an amazing performance with another amazing performance," Devin replied.

"Yeah, I've been worried about that, too. But we have a bigger problem. Kalyn lost her sign. And if we don't find it soon, we're going to be out there spelling 'GO, OLVES' in front of everybody," Emily said.

"*What?*" Devin jumped up from the toilet. "What do you mean, she lost her sign? Where did she leave it?"

"If we knew that, it wouldn't be lost, now, would it?" Emily said. "Come on!"

Devin sighed and followed Emily out of the ladies' room. She couldn't help but think that none of this would be happening if she'd just remembered her lucky socks.

"And next...please give it up for the Northside High School cheerleaders from Sunny Valley, California!" the announcer boomed over the speakers.

Devin and Chloe trotted out to the main floor of the Field House, waving and smiling, as the sixteen other girls followed behind. Kalyn set her sign down next to the others before assuming her position at the edge of the mat. Fortunately, Chloe had found it in the hallway at the last minute, mixed up with blue-and-yellow signs from another high school.

As Devin took her place, she noticed that the special area where the Timberwolves fans were supposed to sit wasn't just occupied by Chloe's, Leila's, and Jenn's parents. The Madison High Spartans JV squad from Akron, Ohio, sat there as well, waving their poms in the air and rooting for the Timberwolves.

Devin couldn't believe it. The Spartans hadn't made it to the finals. Their captain, Di, and the other girls could have chosen to sit in some random spot in the audience or not to be in the Field House at all. But instead, they'd elected to fill in for the missing NHS fans who couldn't make it all the way out to Orlando.

Talk about true spirit, Devin thought.

The music started. Chloe turned and gave her nod to cue the others.

The Spartan squad's kind gesture gave Devin all the confidence she'd been missing just a few hours ago. Smiling and waving happily at them, she launched into her first tumbling pass with renewed faith and energy.

It was nearly ten PM when the NHS JV squad returned to the semicircle on the floor to await the final results. The judges and other officials were taking an unusually long time to tally the scores. During the break, music played on the loudspeakers—a bunch of cheerleaders were standing up and dancing to the song "I Love Rock 'n' Roll" while others remained in their tight huddles.

When the announcer was finally handed the list of winners, Devin turned to Chloe. "This is it," she whispered.

"I know," Chloe replied. "But guess what? Whatever happens, you were a hero tonight. Arianna told me that she spaced and lost count at one point, and that you got her back on track. If you hadn't done that, our entire squad would have been out of sync. We're lucky to have you."

"Thanks, Chloe," Devin said, pleased. She and Chloe had come so far since they first met five months ago. "It really was a team effort, though. You found the missing sign. Kate came through, even though she's sick. The other top girls nailed their liberties. Those girls from Akron, Ohio, rocked! And all this happened without my lucky socks!"

"You have lucky socks?" Chloe said with a laugh.

Devin nodded, blushing.

The two of them fell silent as the announcer began naming teams from the twentieth position on up. Posada High School from Posada, Texas, was in the number twenty spot. George Washington High School from Memphis, Tennessee, had placed at number nineteen. Scott Allen High School from Fort Myers, Florida, was number eighteen.

The names continued, and Northside wasn't among them.

And then...

"Let's make some noise for our fifth-place winners, Northside High School from Sunny Valley, Califoooornia!" the announcer shouted.

Pandemonium ensued as Devin, Chloe, and the rest of their team jumped to their feet and began screaming. They collapsed against one another in a massive group hug, laughing and crying.

Devin and Chloe found each other and shared a high five. Their cocaptaining had paid off.

"Best. Day. Ever," Chloe said as she dabbed at her eyes.

Devin nodded, unable to find her voice. She couldn't imagine a better moment than this.

CHAPTER 20

For Kate, being back in school on Tuesday was surreal. As she walked to her locker before homeroom, total strangers came up to her in the hallway to congratulate her. Glittery hand-painted banners stretched across the halls with messages like CONGRATULATIONS, NHS JV GIRLS! and WAY TO GO, JV CHEERLEADERS! Was it just three days ago that the JV squad had finished in fifth place at Nationals? *Fifth place in the entire country.* The idea still boggled Kate's mind. Their routine hadn't been perfect, and there was room for improvement. Still, fifth place was amazing! Plus, they'd placed just two spots shy of their rivals Breckenridge, who had come in third. The team they'd watched when they first walked into the Field House, Goodrich High from Lexington, Kentucky, had won the national championship.

On Sunday, the NHS squad had watched the Varsity finals the entire day. That night, they'd celebrated at a private party in Hollywood Studios for all the cheerleaders who'd competed at Nationals. Kate normally didn't go for scary rides or roller coasters, but Chloe, Emily, and Devin had persuaded her to try the Tower of Terror and the Rock 'n' Roller Coaster. Kate had kept her eyes squeezed shut and screamed through both rides. Still, a part of her—a very *small* part of her—had enjoyed them. Maybe she was getting braver?

As Kate reached her locker, Emily rushed up, waving excitedly. Kate could tell from her friend's bug-eyed expression that she was already on caffeine overload.

"Hi, Kate! Isn't it a beautiful morning?" Emily called out in a way-too-fast voice. "I didn't sleep at all last night because I was still revved up about Nationals! Plus, I had to make a shopping list for the Valentine's Day dance decorations! Plus, I treated myself to an iced mocha!" She lifted her Disney travel mug to her lips and took a swig.

"Emily, calm down. You should totally pace yourself with that stuff," Kate warned her. "Remember that time you had a massive caffeine crash in third-period bio and fell asleep facedown in a petri dish?"

Emily wrinkled her nose. "Oh, yeah. That wasn't pretty," she murmured. "Which reminds me! You're coming over tonight to make centerpieces, right? Some of the other girls from the Valentine's Day dance committee will be there," she said eagerly.

Kate smiled in confusion. Emily's train of thought was hard to follow. "You mean tonight after practice? I think so." The coach had scheduled a short session in order to "switch gears" from Nationals and get ready for the basketball game against Corning on Friday. "I just have to check with my dad to make sure he doesn't need help with the kids. Otherwise, I should be free," Kate added.

"Awesome! I'll text you to remind you! Oh, hey, there's your boyfriend! Or should I say *ex*-boyfriend! What's going on between you two these days, anyway?" Emily asked, lowering her voice.

Kate whirled around. Adam stood a few feet away, obviously waiting to talk to her. She noticed that he'd gotten a haircut over the long weekend and that he wasn't wearing his glasses.

"Okey-dokey, then. Three's a crowd! Besides, I have a million things to do! See you at practice!" Emily fluttered her fingers and took off.

Alone, Kate and Adam stared at each other for a long moment.

"Hey," Adam said.

Kate didn't respond.

"Contacts," Adam blurted out awkwardly, apparently to explain the absence of his glasses. "I'm not sure I like them, though. It feels like someone's touching my eyeballs."

"Why'd you get them, then?" Kate asked.

"I don't know. But I'm glad I did, because at the least it gives us something to talk about," Adam replied.

"Actually, I need to run. I've got this thing I have to do for Emily before first period," Kate fibbed, glancing over her shoulder.

"Hey, wait a second. What's going on, Kate? Why have you been avoiding me this past week?" Adam asked. "I've texted, e-mailed, and left a billion voice-mail messages. I even left flowers on your doorstep."

Kate had been surprised and pleased to see the bouquet of yellow tulips on her front porch when she got home from the airport yesterday. But her excitement had quickly turned to suspicion. Wasn't that what boys did—make empty gestures to cover up their mistakes? The bouquet had come with a note congratulating her on Nationals and asking her to go to the Valentine's Day dance with him.

"I gave the flowers to your biggest fan, Sasha," she said out loud. "They're on her nightstand, right next to the picture she drew of you with ketchup and green crayon."

"*Please.* Just answer my question. Why are you avoiding me?"

Kate crossed her arms over her chest. "Maybe I'm avoiding you because I can't always tell when you're lying to me," she blurted out.

Adam frowned. "Is that supposed to be some kind of riddle? Because if it is, I don't know the answer."

"Maybe you should ask Willow. She can explain," Kate said coldly.

"*What?* What does Willow have to do with this?" Adam demanded.

Kate's lip trembled, and she felt the hot sting of tears in her eyes. *No.* She wouldn't cry in front of him.

"I really do have to go. Please stop bothering me, okay?" Kate told him.

"*Kate!*"

"And no, I absolutely do not want to go to the Valentine's Day dance with you!"

She didn't wait for his reaction. Instead, she turned and hurried down the hall, hoping and praying that he wouldn't follow her.

He didn't.

CHAPTER 21

"Okay, so the cupcakes, sodas, and bottles of water are a dollar. The big cookies are fifty cents. Those little cookie things are twenty-five cents. Did I forget anything?" Daniel asked Chloe, pointing to the items on the table.

"Those, um, 'little cookie things' aren't actually cookies. They're mini-tarts," Chloe explained. "You know, this totally takes me back to my first day at Hearts Heal, when you were explaining sorting to me."

Daniel laughed. "Yeah, you were a complete newb back then."

It was Saturday night, and the Valentine's Day dance

was about to begin in the Northside High gym. Chloe and Daniel were running the concession table to benefit Hearts Heal. The idea had been Daniel's, and he'd only asked Chloe for some advice about how to arrange the food, but she'd ended up offering to work the table with him for the entire evening. She'd even worn jeans and a HEARTS HEAL T-shirt in lieu of one of her pretty dresses.

Chloe glanced around the gym. She couldn't believe she, Emily, and the other volunteers had managed to transform it into a true-love-themed space in less than a day. The night before, the JV basketball team had played their game against Corning High in here, with Chloe and the rest of the squad cheering Northside on to a 65–42 victory. At seven AM this morning, Emily had dragged Chloe, Devin, Kate, Emily's brother Chris, and a couple of Chris's friends to help set up tables, chairs, and decorations. They'd covered the tables with white crepe paper, pink sequins, flameless candles, and jelly jars filled with frilly red carnations. Mr. Viscardi from the entertainment-equipment rental company had donated a disco ball. Finally, they'd improvised a mini-stage for the DJ and draped it with strings of sparkly lights and big construction-paper hearts.

Emily rushed over to the concession table, waving her clipboard in the air. Her scruffy sneakers and messy ponytail were in stark contrast to her silky black tank dress and strands of faux pearls.

"I know, I know. I need to change into my ballet flats and brush my hair," Emily said, noticing Chloe's curious look. "But I'm in the middle of an emergency. The DJ's not here yet. I've called him and left, like, six messages. What if he doesn't show?"

"Who's the DJ?" Daniel asked curiously.

"My brother Eddie's friend—they call him Mad Dog. They work together at the Mighty Cup. He DJs part-time and also plays keyboard for a band in Torrance Heights." Emily glanced impatiently at her watch. "*Ugh!* Why are musicians so unreliable? No offense, Daniel. Oh, there he is! Gotta go!" She hurried off.

"I get dizzy just listening to her," Daniel remarked to Chloe.

Chloe giggled. "I know. She's amazing and she always gets the job done."

"Hey, speaking of which . . . I'm okay doing the concessions by myself tonight. You probably want to hang out with your friends. Or dance with your boyfriend or whatever." Daniel dropped his gaze to the table and switched two trays of cupcakes around, then switched them back again.

"Um . . . I don't have a boyfriend. And I like hanging out with you. Besides, how can I leave you alone? You don't know the difference between cookies and mini-tarts," Chloe teased him.

"Ha-ha. So how is it that someone as smart and pretty as you doesn't have a boyfriend?" Daniel grinned and shook his head. "Sorry, that sounded like a total pickup line, didn't it? I didn't mean it like that."

Chloe blushed, secretly pleased by the compliment. "That's okay. I'm not sure. Maybe because I've been too busy for boys?"

"Yeah. I've kind of been too busy for girls. I guess we have a lot in common that way," Daniel told her.

Chloe gazed up at him. He was so cute. And nice. And passionate about what he believed in, just like her. For a moment, she wondered if he was going to ask her out....

"Mini-tart?" he said, offering her a plate.

Or not. "Only if you're paying," she joked.

Daniel dropped a quarter into the cash jar, then split one of the mini-tarts and handed half to Chloe. She thought: *What if Daniel did ask me out? Would I say yes? They* were from such different worlds. She was a cheerleader at Northside. He was a violin prodigy at Sunny Valley Performing Arts.

"Yeah, so I was wondering if you were free next—" Daniel began.

"Yes!" Chloe said immediately.

"Really?"

"Really."

Chloe couldn't wait to tell Emily and the others.

178

By seven thirty, the event was in full swing. Emily looked on as a mob of students danced on the floor to one of Mad Dog's excellent hip-hop mixes. The disco ball spun slowly and shimmered like silver stardust. Couples sat at the tables holding hands and eating pink cupcakes and heart-shaped cookies.

"Ems!"

Emily turned around and saw Travis walking toward her. He looked especially hot tonight in a vintage black tuxedo jacket and faded gray Soul Alignment T-shirt over his usual skinny jeans.

Travis put his hands on Emily's shoulders and kissed her lightly on the lips. He tasted yummy, like peppermint. "Great dance. You really know how to throw a party," he told her, brushing his long blond bangs out of his eyes.

"Thanks! I've been nonstop since Tuesday pulling it together. I'm sorry I missed rehearsal yesterday," Emily apologized.

"No worries. You're totally ready for tomorrow's recording session. Alex and I changed this one section on 'Blue,' but we can go over it with you on the car ride there. Oh, and Jacinta moved back the start time, so I'll be picking you up at eleven AM, not ten."

Emily hesitated. "About that..." she began.

Travis frowned. "What? Is the later time going to be a problem?"

"Noooo." Emily took a deep breath. "So there's something I have to tell you. Before I left for Nationals, I talked to my parents about joining Hashtag, the meeting with Jacinta, everything."

"And?"

"They were totally *not* cool with it. They were okay with me singing with you guys once in a while, for fun. But they didn't want me to even *think* about doing it professionally until I'm older."

Travis stared at her incredulously. "Wait, *what*? You're telling me this *now*? On the eve of the most important recording session of our lives? Rampage is deciding whether to sign us based on our performance tomorrow," he snapped.

Emily held up her hands. "I know, I know. But listen, Travis...I'm not finished. At first, I was desperately trying to find a way to make my mom and dad change their minds. Or figure out a compromise that would make them and you and me happy. And I think I came up with a solution."

"What?" Travis asked suspiciously.

"I'll sing with you guys tomorrow. That way, you can show off Hashtag's songwriting and performance skills with a female vocalist in the mix," Emily explained. "After tomorrow, I'll step aside, and you can find another female vocalist to sing with Hashtag. In fact, I had an idea. Did you know that Serena Davenport has a little cousin who goes to Sunny Valley Performing Arts? Her name is Sophie Davenport. I found her online. She's sixteen, and she sings. I watched some of her home videos on YouTube, and she's really good. She has exactly the sort of soulful, edgy sound you're looking for. *And* she has the Davenport name."

Travis didn't respond. He stuffed his hands into his pockets and exhaled angrily.

"I really love singing. But I'm not ready to decide if that's what I want to do for the rest of my life," Emily went on, trying to make him understand. "I also realized something else, while I was at Nationals. I'm not ready to give up cheering. I only have three years left to cheer for the Timberwolves, assuming I make it through tryouts in April, and then maybe another four years in college. If I'm still interested in a singing career then, I can always pursue it after I graduate."

"Are you delusional, Emily? This is a once-in-a-lifetime deal. Rampage likes you *today*. There's a good chance they're not going to feel the same way about you next month or next year or seven years from now, because some-one better's gonna come along—someone prettier and more talented," Travis pointed out.

Ouch. "Okay. I guess that's fair. But I'm willing to take that chance," Emily told him bluntly.

Travis pulled his phone out of his jacket pocket and began scrolling. "Whatever. Look. Forget about recording with us tomorrow. I think I know someone who can fill in for you."

"Really? Who?"

"Doesn't matter. Hashtag's not your concern anymore. Good-bye, Emily." Travis turned to go.

"Wait, Travis!" Emily put her hand on his arm. "We're still okay, right? I mean, you and me?"

"Seriously? There *is* no you and me without Hashtag. You really *are* delusional, aren't you?"

Travis took off. Emily stared after him in shock. Had he just broken up with her? And basically told her that he'd strung her along? That he'd made her believe he liked her just so that she would sing with the group?

CHAPTER 22

Devin sat at the ticket table, watching couples head onto the dance floor as the DJ put on a slow, romantic song by Calla called "Meant to Be." It was past eight, so no one else was coming through the door to buy tickets, which left Devin free to get up and party with her friends.

But she wasn't in the mood to dance. The electric excitement she'd felt at Nationals after the team's fifth-place win was starting to fade. It was back to reality now, which meant making up the couple of quizzes she'd missed while in Orlando. And dealing with her mom's fury over the news that Devin's dad had started dating someone from his office. And having to take Emerald to the emergency vet clinic two nights ago because she wouldn't stop throwing up. (Thankfully, she was fine now.)

And, of course, there was Josh.

They had Skyped last night after the Corning game, since it was officially Valentine's Day. He'd caught her up on the news about his little sister. Josie was doing well, and Josh's family had found a preschool that would meet her needs.

They'd also talked about Nationals and Josh's new pet turtle and his family's upcoming camping trip to Yosemite.

At one point, Devin had come so close to telling him about Mateo. To telling him that she'd developed feelings for another guy and wanted to take some time to figure out what it meant. But she hadn't been able to bring herself to do it, especially after Josh told her that he really, really missed her and that he had a special Valentine's surprise for her.

Devin had no idea what the surprise might be. Nothing had come in the mail today. Maybe he was composing a new song for her? They had another Skype date set for later tonight.

"Hey, Devin."

Devin glanced up, startled. Mateo was standing there. He looked incredibly handsome in a white button-down shirt and faded jeans. His curly black hair was slightly slicked back.

"Oh, hey, Mateo!" Devin picked up a pen and began scribbling random numbers on her notepad in an effort to appear busy. "I was just adding up tonight's receipts. How are you? Are you having fun?" she babbled.

"I guess. What about you?"

"You know. Just working. Hey, great game last night!"

She felt stupid making silly small talk with Mateo, but she couldn't help it. She didn't want him to know that she'd been thinking about him just now. And all day. And yesterday. And the day before.

"Thanks. So, um, I didn't see you much this week," Mateo said awkwardly.

"What do you mean? We saw each other in history class," Devin pointed out.

"That's not what I meant. You canceled our study hall session. Is everything okay?"

"Yes. I'm so sorry. I, um, had this other thing I had to do. But I promise I'll get back on track with our mock-trial project. I know it's due in a couple of weeks."

"I'm not worried about the mock-trial project. I know we'll get it done. It's just that..." Mateo looked away.

"What?"

"I wanted to ask you to the dance. To *this* dance, I mean," he blurted out.

Devin's breath caught in her throat. "You did?"

"Yeah, big-time. But I was scared you'd say no. You've kind of been avoiding me lately. You're not exactly an easy person to read, Devin Isle."

Devin stared up at him. He looked so vulnerable just then. *Omigosh*, Devin realized. *He feels the same way I do.*

She grinned shyly and held out her hand. "Okay. Yes."

Mateo glanced down at her in surprise. "What did you say?"

"I said yes, I'll go to this dance with you."

Mateo gave her a dazzling smile and gently clasped her hand in his. She stood up and walked around the table to join him. He pulled her in close as they began swaying to the Calla song, right then and there.

Devin closed her eyes and rested her head against Mateo's chest. His arms were warm and strong where they held her, and his skin smelled like Ivory soap.

Devin was finally ready to admit that she had a crush on Mateo and wanted to spend more time with him.

The song switched to a faster tempo. Devin opened her eyes...

...and saw Josh standing in the gym doorway, holding

a single red rose in his hand. Watching her and Mateo with a stunned expression.

❋

By the time Devin made her excuses to Mateo and ran outside, she found Josh sitting on a bench near the parking lot. He was plucking the petals from the rose one by one and letting them flutter to the ground.

Devin sat down next to him, trying to shake off her shock and guilt. How could she have let this happen?

"I am so, so sorry!" she began miserably.

"So much for my big Valentine's surprise, huh, Devver?" Josh said without looking at her.

"I should have told you before. I'm such a jerk. Will you ever forgive me?" she pleaded.

Josh shrugged. "You know what? I'm kind of glad this happened."

Devin startled. "You are?"

"I think we've both been kidding ourselves for a while now."

"We have?"

"I care about you, and you care about me. I think. But the long-distance thing sucks. We can't make this work when we can only see each other every couple of months," Josh pointed out.

"I know. It does suck. But I should have been honest with you," Devin admitted.

Josh bent forward to pick up a couple of rose petals from the ground. He turned them over in his hand. "So... how long have you been dating him? That guy in there," he asked after a moment.

"Oh, Mateo? We haven't been dating. He's just a friend. We're not even here at the dance together. Not really, anyway. We were just, uh..." Devin fumbled for the right words.

"It's okay. You don't need to explain. Come on, let me walk you back in. I'm going to call our family friends who live nearby. I can stay with them tonight and then take the bus back to Spring Park tomorrow morning."

"Oh, Josh! I'm so sorry that you came all the way down here for this!"

"It's okay, Devver. I'll survive. Besides, I can always write a song about it. Maybe call it 'The Valentine's Day Dance Blues.'" Josh tried to make a joke.

Devin started to cry.

"Hey, stop that. You're going to make me cry, too," Josh told her, brushing her tears away with the back of his hand.

Devin took a moment to compose herself and dab at her face. When she and Josh finally headed back inside the gym, Mateo was waiting for her near the doorway.

Mateo's glance bounced curiously between Devin and Josh. "Is everything okay?" he asked Devin.

Josh stepped forward and stuck out his hand. "I'm Josh, Devin's friend from her old school," he said with a smile, letting Devin know that he'd be okay. "But I actually have somewhere to be. It was good to see you, Devin. I'll tell Nina and Cameron that you said hey...."

❋

Kate stood at the ticket table as she divided the money in the cash box into ones, fives, tens, twenties, and change. She'd offered to finish up so Devin could enjoy the rest of the dance with Mateo.

She peered around the crowded gym. People seemed to be having fun. The music was great. The decorations looked beautiful. Chloe and Daniel were at the concession table, joking and laughing nonstop. Devin and Mateo were talking with their heads bent close. And Emily was dancing with Gemma, Lexi, and a bunch of other girls from the cheer squad.

"Is the dance still going on?"

Someone handed her a ticket. Kate glanced up in surprise.

It was Adam, looking cute in a button-down shirt and navy-blue tie.

Kate stared at the ticket in her hand and realized

quickly that it wasn't actually a ticket at all. It was a tiny rolled-up scroll with a red ribbon tied around it.

"Go ahead, read it," Adam said.

Kate hesitated, then untied the ribbon carefully and flattened the scroll in the palm of her hand.

It was written in Adam's neat, old-fashioned cursive. It said:

"The course of true love never did run smooth."
                                    —William Shakespeare
P.S. I talked to Willow. She made up the whole thing because she wanted you and me to break up.
P.P.S. Can you give me another chance?
P.P.P.S. I miss you.

Kate raised her head slowly. "B-b-but why did she want to break us up?"

"She lied about having a big fat crush on Sebastian the tennis player. I guess she had a big fat crush on me, and she always has. I was totally oblivious. I'm sorry she pulled her crazy act on you," Adam apologized.

Relieved, Kate hugged Adam. He hugged her back.

"So are we okay?" Adam whispered in her ear.

"We're totally okay," Kate replied.

"Good! Although it's becoming a tradition with us, Kate. This is the second dance in a row where we've had some awful, awkward misunderstanding. The spring dance is in May. We'll have to come up with another awful, awkward misunderstanding so that we can make up halfway through *that* one, too," Adam joked.

Kate laughed and hugged him again.

All's well that ends well, she thought happily.

CHAPTER 23

"Who wants popcorn?" Chloe called out as she walked into her bedroom, balancing a tray loaded high with snacks. Her dog, Valentine, sat up from her napping spot and eyed the food hungrily.

"Is it kettle corn or buttered?" Emily asked, twisting her hair up in a clip.

"I vote for nacho cheese," Devin said, rolling her sleeping bag out on the floor.

Kate pulled on a pink hoodie over her white tank top. "Mmm, nacho cheese. I second that," she piped up.

"We've got kettle corn, buttered, *and* nacho cheese. That should make everyone happy," Chloe announced. She tried not to spill anything on her new baby-blue pajamas as she set the heavy tray down on her bed.

It was almost midnight on Saturday. The four girls had decided at the last minute to have a sleepover at Chloe's house after the Valentine's Day dance. They'd all agreed that they needed to seriously decompress from their long, exhausting week. And for the first time in weeks, there was no cheer practice on Sunday, so they could spend the entire day in their pj's, watching DVDs and giving each other mani-pedis.

Chloe was really looking forward to chilling out with her friends. She was especially glad to have Devin there as part of the group. It was important for the two of them to be friends, especially with cheer tryouts coming up in April and summer camp just around the corner. Chloe had no idea whether they would be cocaptains next season. But whatever happened, she and Devin needed to be able to work together as one to make the Timberwolves the best squad it could be.

Devin reached over and grabbed a handful of nacho cheese popcorn. "So, Kate—are you and Adam okay now? I saw you dancing together," she said.

Kate smiled and nodded. *Yes yes yes.* "We're totally okay!"

"What about that girl Willow? Is she going to leave you two alone?" Chloe asked curiously.

"Adam had a long talk with her. She *says* she'll leave us alone. But even if she doesn't, I trust Adam. I know he wouldn't do anything to hurt me," Kate replied.

"Wow, it's ironic, isn't it? I'm the only one of us who's single now," Emily remarked.

"Excuse me? I'm totally single. I just broke up with Josh, like, a few hours ago," Devin pointed out.

"Yeah, and you spent the rest of the night slow-dancing with Mateo Torres. He was holding you, like, *this close* the entire time." Emily gestured with two pieces of popcorn.

"Stop it!" Devin said, laughing but blushing furiously. "We're just friends. For now." She picked up one of Chloe's heart-shaped pillows and hugged it to her chest. She was still sad about Josh, but she was strangely relieved, too. At the same time, just thinking about Mateo made her feel warm and giddy inside.

Chloe raised her hand. "Well, *I'm* still single, too."

"Yeah, but not for long. When are you and Daniel going out on your big date?" Kate asked eagerly.

Chloe beamed. "Next Saturday. He's taking me to a concert at his school. I can't wait!"

"You watch, Chloe. Now that you're unavailable, Greg Marina is totally going to ask you out," Emily predicted. "It's what guys do. They want you when they can't have you. They pretend to be your boyfriend so they can use you for something they really want, like a recording contract."

"Awww, Em." Chloe reached over and squeezed her hand. "Are you okay about what happened? Do you want us to yell at Travis for you?"

"I'm fine. I just feel stupid about falling for his sleazy act," Emily admitted.

"So no regrets? About not joining Hashtag?" Kate asked.

Emily plopped back against the pillows and studied her nails. "Nope, no regrets. *Welllll*...maybe just the tiniest little bit. I mean, I could have been riding around town in limousines instead of in my parents' boring minivan. Or hanging out at the Grammys with Calla and that hot guy from the Blue Skinks. Or finally having the money to upgrade Chad." She looked up and grinned. "But mostly, I'm just glad that I can be with you guys when we rock Nationals next year. I *so* want those white satin jackets the national champions get!"

The four girls laughed. Chloe pumped her fist in the air. "To Nationals!" she saluted.

Emily, Kate, and Devin joined in. "To Nationals!"